THE WILD HEAVENS

SARAH LOUISE BUTLER

THE WILD HEAVENS

A NOVEL

Douglas & McIntyre

Douglas and McIntyre (2013) Ltd.
P.O. Box 219, Madeira Park, BC, VON 2HO
www.douglas-mcintyre.com

Edited by Pam Robertson
Cover design by Anna Comfort O'Keeffe
Text design by Brianna Cerkiewicz
Printed and bound in Canada
Printed on 100 percent recycled paper

Canada Council   Conseil des arts
for the Arts   du Canada

BRITISH COLUMBIA   BRITISH
ARTS COUNCIL   COLUMBIA
Supported by the Province of British Columbia

Canada

Douglas and McIntyre (2013) Ltd. acknowledges the support of the
Canada Council for the Arts, the Government of Canada, and the
Province of British Columbia through the BC Arts Council.

Library and Archives Canada Cataloguing in Publication

Title: The wild heavens / Sarah Louise Butler.

Names: Butler, Sarah Louise, 1975- author.

Identifiers: Canadiana (print) 20190217669 | Canadiana (ebook)
    20190217677 | ISBN 9781771622585 (softcover) | ISBN 9781771622592
    (HTML)

Classification: LCC PS8603.U863 W55 2020 | DDC C813/.6—dc23

For my parents, Margaret Taylor Butler and Peter Eugene Butler; for botany and Latin and everything else

PROLOGUE

IN EARLY WINTER OF 1920, a young seminarian crouched in the snow before an impossible set of tracks. Their familiar shape, their massive size—the conjunction of the two properties simply defied reason. Each footprint was nearly twice the length of his boot, yet each showed a round heel, a raised arch, an inside toe considerably larger than the other four. But for their size, it was as though he himself had foolishly wandered out in bare feet. He brushed his fingers through the fresh snow inside one of the deep prints: just a dusting. Whoever or whatever made them couldn't be far away.

His scalp prickled. He stood and looked warily around. Cedar-forested mountains rose up all around him; the only discernible movement was the falling snow. The trail led out of the clearing, then wove through the trees and out of sight.

Snowflakes alighted briefly on his cheeks and dissolved. Far off, a Steller's jay called out in its unlovely voice; a distant woodpecker drummed against dead wood. Fluffy clusters of flakes fell densely, straight down, in the tireless, unhurried manner of heavy snow under calm winds. The trail would be covered within hours.

The young man, Aidan Fitzpatrick, followed the line of tracks as they traversed the densely forested mountainside and began to climb. The shape of the footprints became less clear as the snow deepened on the ascent, and he started to question what he had seen until they passed through the thinner snow beneath the draped skirts of a towering cedar. Their form was, again, clearly revealed, as utterly inexplicable as they'd been at valley bottom.

He crested a ridge and froze in place, heart pounding. It was right there in its own tracks, not twenty yards away. Covered in grizzled brown fur, it stood upright, broad-shouldered and a good nine feet tall. It turned to face him, revealing features that were both simian and human, then it regarded him with a calm, perceptive curiosity. The young seminarian could only stare mutely, his fear held loosely—ready to grasp but at arm's length—because his primary impression was not that the creature was frightening, but that it was magnificent. It was impossible, and yet there it stood. His right hand twitched up to cross himself, but he stilled it. His legs felt suddenly weak and he fought the impulse to fall to his knees.

What is this? By what grace am I offered this sight? He was startled to feel the warmth of tears in his eyes and the creature saw this, too. It took a step forward and he closed his eyes, imagined its massive hand gentle against his cheek. The cry of a raven pierced the silence. He opened his eyes as the creature turned and loped away, striding so elegantly on its two legs that he felt an undeniable sense of kinship and reached out his hand. It moved swiftly through the trees and disappeared. He rushed forward, raced along its tracks until they stopped above a low cliff; for as far as he could see, the snow beyond was unmarked. He looked up at the snow-encased trees that surrounded him, but he could see no sign of the creature. There was only the clear, single line of tracks, leading nowhere.

The young man stood among those snow-ghost trees, looking out over the valley. Nothing moved. *That was no animal. And yet, neither was it a man.* Man and beast were on different planes, separated from each other not only by the trappings of civilization but by an existential and clearly defined wall; how, then, could such a creature exist? So much like us, so much like them? He pondered the sense of affinity he had felt at seeing it walk, and knew that it was not whimsy but a reordering of taxonomy as he had understood it, which naturally begged the question— he paused, Darwin and the book of Genesis sparring in his thoughts—then shook his head.

His damp undershirt clung to his skin. Each exhalation was visible in the cold, still air and the snow continued, soft and persistent. A chill began to seep through his heavy pants and sweaters, and he turned away and began the long walk down the mountain, weighing his allegiances, negotiating compromises. He was struck with the vertiginous realization that the foundations of his faith were crumbling beneath him, and he lost his footing and tumbled downslope, landing on his wool-swathed backside in the snow.

The forest around him was profoundly quiet. Snowflakes dusted his eyelashes and out of old habit he looked up, imagining he could discern their source, but there was only the grey backdrop of sky and the seemingly infinite whiteness moving toward him, and whether the falling snow materialized from a few yards above or from the heavens themselves, he couldn't say. He knew only that perfect stellar snowflakes continued to settle on his ungracefully sprawled form, and that the cedars rising up around him would persevere long after man and his foolishness, that their dense boughs sheltered tiny chickadees, their feathers fluffed against the cold, their tiny hearts beating fiercely. He knew there were men who could make peace with a God who was not Creator, and he knew himself to be no such man.

He stood, brushed himself off and continued down toward the valley bottom, along the mingled tracks of the miraculous creature's feet and his own boots. As he walked, he began to prepare the necessary explanations for his confessor and his fellow seminarians and, God help him, his elderly parents.

A week after the encounter, Aidan Joseph Fitzpatrick stood, for the last time, outside the stone building that had been his home through years of study. The wind was cold and he felt it carried, somehow, the disappointment of his peers and superiors, the dashed hopes of his parents and even the weighty shadows of his ancestors, those threadbare and half-starved Irish farmers who arrived on this continent carrying little but the faith their great-grandson would lose forever in a patch of fresh snow. A gust lifted his hat from his head, he chased it down and the brief motion warmed him—he felt again his own convictions, fresh and untested but right there with him, as close as his warm and beating heart.

He stepped onto a westbound train in the Interior mountains of British Columbia and emerged the next morning on the Pacific coast, where he would enroll in a secular university to study biology. His knowledge of Latin gave him the disorienting but not unpleasant impression that he had stepped sideways into a parallel world, one where faith was meaningless and evidence everything but somehow the language was just the same. After graduation, he continued his studies and became a veterinarian. He saved for years to buy the chunk of raw land where he'd first seen the tracks, then moved back to the Interior and started on a cabin. After a year of travelling widely for work, he took a teaching position at a university some hours north. He found that it suited him, and began to spend much of each year there, returning in the spring and summer to the unfinished cabin, to the land that was beginning to feel like his home.

When the cabin was finally built, he dragged a nine-foot length of cedar into the clearing and began, painstakingly, to carve. He managed a decent replica of the creature's body, but finally conceded his struggle to reproduce the impossible nuances of its countenance. He stood the flawed sculpture inside the doorway of his new home and it brought him satisfaction each time he saw it—at first despite, then later because of, its imperfection. It seemed fitting that the creature could not be so easily captured.

He married and had one daughter. She, in turn, would have one child: his only granddaughter, a slight, willful girl who would grow into a woman with a secret.

My origins include not only that young seminarian but also the creature who, at little more than a glance, turned him from his proscribed path of Catholic priesthood and celibacy. Had my grandfather, Aidan

Fitzpatrick, not happened upon those tracks in the snow in 1920, it is unlikely that I would ever have been born.

PART ONE

ONE

2003

LAST NIGHT'S SNOWSTORM HAS BLANKETED the forest in quiet. In the loft of my cabin, I dream of my late husband, Luke. We stand in a forest clearing on a winter night, and he turns toward me. As he opens his mouth to speak, I am awakened by a noise from downstairs.

Early morning light bathes the loft. Still hazy, I think, *mouse.* The sound has that light flitting quality of something alive, almost weightless and in rapid motion. I try to fall back asleep but the gentle racket from downstairs persists. I sit up. It's not a rodent. Its movement is more swishing, fluttery, as though a large tropical moth has strayed thousands of miles north of its range into the Interior of British Columbia.

I leave my bed and climb down the ladder to the main floor. A fox sparrow has inexplicably found its way inside and is flying lightly and repeatedly at the one window in the cabin that can't be opened. I open the door and stand back; this has been effective with the bats that occasionally find their way indoors on summer nights. The sparrow, lacking the bats' ability to echolocate, continues trying to escape through the glass. I move forward, thinking to catch it in my hands, but then I retreat to lift a thin cardigan from the hook. The preoccupied bird seems not to notice my approach and I swiftly enfold it in the sweater, making a gentle shushing noise in an attempt to convey that I am not a threat, the same soft *shh-shh-shh* I calmed the kids with when they were babies. The sparrow goes still, but I can feel the thrum of its pulse as I carry it to the open door. One fragile, toothpick leg sticks out from the woollen bundle and I obey an irrational impulse to tuck it neatly back in.

I stand at the open doorway in the muted light of a landscape draped in fresh snow, and unwrap the sweater. There is a moment when one sharp claw is caught, held by a wisp of wool, and then the sparrow tugs free. It flies off, over a single line of massive tracks that bisects the clearing, marking the passing of a visitor I haven't seen sign of in decades.

My heart clenches. The sight of these tracks awakens a hope I only now realize I've been holding on to, clutching it so long and so tightly that surely the passage of time should have killed it by now, if not my suffocating grip. I hardly dare to look away as I pull on a pair of boots. My steps are silent on the snow as I move closer. I crouch before one of the tracks, lean in and blow forceful, directed huffs of air onto its snow-dusted surface. The fresh, dry snow disperses in a white cloud, revealing an apparently human footprint that is twice as long as my boot.

I spread my fingers to set them into the smoothness of the toeprints. Something flits in front of me and I look up to see a whiskey jack settling onto a cedar bough at the forest edge. It watches me intently, as though I might unearth something that would be of interest to us both.

I stand, shivering in my nightdress. The trail skirts around the gnarled apple tree, then crosses the clearing and disappears into the cedars. I walk up the cabin steps, mentally preparing a checklist. Snowshoes and collapsible ski poles, the emergency kit and both thermoses, filled with hot, honeyed tea. I'll need trail food, nothing that will freeze solid in my pack, and my own winter boots, not this old pair of Luke's I've pulled on, two sizes too big and broken open at the toe. They are really no use at all anymore, but I haven't yet managed to throw them away.

The cabin door creaks as I open it. The wooden sculpture stands inside the door like a sentry, its features suggestive of man and ape and god, all at once. The feet are oversized, even for its considerable height; it looms over me as I rush around the cabin retrieving items to stuff into my pack.

The creature, whose image my grandfather held in his mind as he carved, has been called many things, but Grandpa feared the inevitable day that one of us would let its name slip, revealing in an instant what he had dedicated a lifetime to keeping secret. So, for our purposes, I was taught to call it, to call all of them, "Charlie," and I have continued to do so. Always Charlie, although at least one was male and another certainly female, and although the individual that passed through these hills in 1920 was likely not the same one whose tracks I came upon as a young girl in the 1960s—which was itself perhaps not the one Luke tracked so many years later.

I pause at the coat hooks. I have kept just one of Luke's old coats, an insulated wool parka, and I am tempted to bring it now but it's too bulky to pack, and too warm for the exertion of what will surely be an uphill climb. I leave it on the hook and pull on my own jacket and boots, swing my loaded pack onto my back and tighten the straps. I reach up to touch the smooth wood of Charlie's broad chest. His eyes stare straight ahead and he looks at once anguished and resigned, as though he knows a terrible secret, the revelation of which will change nothing. I slip on my gloves and leave the warmth of the cabin, cross the porch and step down into the snow.

I follow the tracks across the clearing and beneath the heavy canopy of cedars, where the fresh snow has only lightly penetrated and the marks of each toe are clearly visible. I follow them downslope, roughly following the trail to the lake, through cedar and hemlock, past the dead, frozen stalks of devil's club and thimbleberry and the bare branches of aspen. My spinning thoughts have distilled into two sharp points, and they march alongside me in their own rhythm. *Charlie. Luke. Luke, Charlie. Charlie, Luke.* I walk quickly, setting a pace I won't be able to keep. Through the trees, I can see the white expanse of the lake, spread out across the valley bottom.

I met Luke when we were both seven years old. I can still see him as he was then: his open, expectant face, his narrow chest and skinny, little-boy arms. He looks back at me; I can see everything that will come to pass between us and I hesitate, unable to decide whether to let it spool out the same way again, or to turn from him and walk away. His eyes beseech me to believe the impossible words forming on his lips. It was right here on this beach, in late August of 1959.

TWO

I STEPPED OFF THE PORCH and out into the warm air, a wiry, freckled child squinting in the late afternoon sun. Steep, forested mountains wrapped around the cabin in all directions but one. Downslope from the clearing, the cedar forest was shot through with sparkling flashes of sunlight glinting off the small lake that filled the narrow valley bottom. The sun warmed my bare arms as I plucked seeds, one by one, from the nodding, yellow-ringed head of a stunted sunflower that would never grow taller than me, despite enjoying the sunniest spot in the clearing. I slipped the seeds into the back pocket of my jeans and ducked under the cedar boughs onto the worn dirt path that led to the lake.

It was cooler under the ceiling of trees. A jay's raucous call rang out and I stopped, scanning until I spotted it perched on a tree; its shape familiar but its plumage blue and black, instead of blue and white like the ones back home in Ontario. The day before, Grandpa had told me its full name but I couldn't recall it, so I tested myself on the names of the plants living on the forest floor. Falsebox, with toothy leaves like my new front tooth coming in, prince's pine—not princess, as I'd thought before. Western teaberry, with its rare, cinnamon-tasting red berries, and rattlesnake plantain, which had been a disappointment when Grandpa showed it to me, as it bore no resemblance to any kind of snake. I thought of the garter snakes back home, my mother pointing one out to me, telling me not to be afraid as I shrank back against the comfort of her body. Now I felt a stab of fear, thinking of her, and I moved more quickly along the trail.

I stopped and crouched before the live squirrel trap I'd woven yesterday from flexible young branches. I peered inside: nothing. I dug the sunflower seeds out of my pocket and laid them out in a trail, leading to the trap. While waiting for the squirrels to notice my offering, I concocted furnishings for them from bits of moss and wood. Occasionally I hooted softly to attract owls, until it occurred to me that my hooting was doing little to endear me to the squirrels. I continued down the trail until I'd nearly reached the lake, then held seeds on my outstretched hands and tried to lure the chickadees from the shrubby dogwood and snowberry that grew between forest and beach. I imagined the birds' slight weight, their feet scratchy against my palms. One had a damaged foot— the clawed toes were misshapen into a ball of tissue; the bird seemed untroubled but I was determined to take it home and nurse it back to health, regardless. The word *home* had a blurred, unsettled edge to it; this was to be my home now, the cabin and Grandpa. I'd been here three days already, each morning waking disoriented in my loft bedroom in the cabin, but it still seemed impossible.

The chickadees chattered to each other, and took no notice of me. My arms ached and I had to lower them. I left the shelter of the trees and stepped out onto the pebbly shoreline. Near the mouth of the creek a boy stood on the beach, looking out at the water. A fishing rod and bucket lay on the ground between us. Had Grandpa said something about a boy? I was still in a daze from the sudden changes that had overtaken my life, and couldn't recall for certain.

"Who are you?" I asked. He turned and looked at me.

"Well, I'm *really* an eagle," he said. "I was asleep in my nest and I had a dream I was a juvenile male human, and now I'm stuck like this."

He was wearing cut-off jean shorts; he had blue eyes and his dark hair needed cutting. "You look like a regular boy," I said.

"My nice, sharp talons turned into feet, and my wings turned into these," he said. He lifted both arms, regarded them with some distaste and slowly lowered them.

"I'm waiting here because I can't fly home." He peered up into the sky as a mature bald eagle glided over the lake. "There's my dad, my real one. He must be wondering where I am."

"That one?" I asked. I lifted my finger to point but he put his hand on my arm and very gently pushed it down.

"Don't point at him," he said, shaking his head. "Eagles hate being pointed at."

The eagle circled, made a splashy attempt to catch a fish. It soared back up, talons empty.

"I know he's looking for me," he said, "but he'll never recognize me, until I change back to an eagle."

"When will you change back?" I asked.

"Whenever I wake up from the dream." He shrugged and looked more closely at me, at my long, blonde braids and bare feet.

"How old are you?" he asked.

I told him, seven, and he smiled.

"If you were an eagle, you'd already be an adult," he said. "You'd have your white head and tail feathers. Probably even a few eaglets, by now."

I noticed his tan line where his shorts were hanging low. The detail seemed at odds with his story. "How old are *you*?"

The boy didn't answer. Instead, he flexed his toes experimentally and said, "I don't know how you humans manage to catch *anything* with these soft little talons."

I indicated the fishing rod and bucket lying on the pebbles. "Why do you need a fishing rod, if you're an eagle?"

He looked at the rod as if noticing it for the first time. "Not mine," he said, and took a quick step away from it.

"If you're really an eagle," I asked, "Why do you know how to talk like a person?"

"Do you ever have a dream where you can fly?" he asked. "Same exact thing."

I considered that for a moment.

"Do you want to catch squirrels with me?" I asked, finally.

"You mean, to eat?" He wrinkled his nose. "I'm a *bald* eagle, not a golden."

"Not to *eat*," I said. "To take care of. Teach them things, maybe."

"Eagles don't keep other animals for pets," he said. "*Nobody* does, except you humans."

I stared at him a moment, then turned away and walked along the beach. I dug a hole near the shoreline and watched it fill with water. I glanced over at the boy; he was piling flattish stones on top of each other until they toppled. The eagle was scanning the lake again and we both watched as it looped back behind the mountains. When it disappeared from view, the boy slumped down on the ground and lowered his head against his knees. I looked at him for a moment, then approached cautiously and squatted beside him. He looked up and his face was streaked with tears.

"That wasn't really him," he said, quietly. "My real dad is gone."

Immediately, accidentally, I thought again of my mother. We had stood here together, when I was five, and probably when I was three as well. We had planned to come here later this summer—both of us, together. My heart sped up, my throat dried and I couldn't speak.

"He flew straight into the propeller of an airplane," the boy said, and shook his head. "Feathers *everywhere*."

He jumped up and ran off down the beach, flapping his arms like wings.

I watched until he slipped into the forest. I got back to digging, widening the hole into a trench that reached the lake. I lost track of time, until the sun started to slip behind the mountains and the air was suddenly cool. I stood, brushed the sand from my knees and followed the path up from the lake. Overhead, the crows were all flying home. Nothing in the squirrel trap. I ducked under the trailing cedar boughs and there was the cabin. The door creaked as I opened it; there were no lamps on so it was darker inside than out. Grandpa wasn't there, just a note saying he had gone for a walk.

The strange wooden sculpture that Grandpa called "Charlie" looked different in the low light. I dragged a chair over to where it stood inside the door of the cabin, and climbed up. From this perspective I could study its features, and I saw that its expression was sad. More than sad: it looked as though it was the loneliest creature on earth. I reached up and touched the corner of its eye, imagined finding a hidden tear there.

My mother was not here. But I knew she was not four days away by train, either, inside the long, frightening box they'd put her in. She couldn't be buried in a hole, its edges showing the severed roots of grass that was so lush and perfect it could hardly be real. It had been more than a week; surely, by now, she had escaped. She would be tracking me as she flew north over the train tracks that had brought me here, over the ripening corn and leafy green trees to where the rocks stood up sharp and straight alongside the tracks, then over the pine-fringed lakes and the dark boggy forests of black spruce, and west across the endless wheat fields. She was crossing over the Rockies, and soon she would glide across the lake to circle over the cabin, her white head and tail feathers shining, preparing to land, to wake me up and take me home.

THREE

A RAVEN CALLS OUT FROM high in a tree, startling me back to the present. A response echoes back from across the frozen lake and I turn to see the bird lift off above me, a dark shadow in the grey sky. The lake is covered in snow, and the expanse of white gives off a dull glow despite the overcast morning. The scene before me is of silence and stillness, and it would be easy to assume that nothing lives beneath that thick sheet of ice and snow. I turn away and step back under the cover of the trees. Charlie's trail skirts the edge of the beach and disappears into the forest. I hitch up my pack, tighten the straps and follow.

FOUR

A DISTANT SOUND PULLED ME from sleep, and I sat up in bed. There was a faint glow of moonlight through the window in my loft. It was 1961, and I was nine years old.

The sound came again, an eerie call echoing around the mountains that surrounded the cabin. It built up then faded out, a bit like a wolf's howl but deeper, less sustained. Not any bird I could think of. Not *anything* I could think of. My arms prickled, and I felt a chill under the wool blankets I'd wrapped around myself. I strained to hear Grandpa snoring in his bedroom downstairs, but the cabin was quiet. I called to him, waited.

I climbed down the ladder, stood in his bedroom doorway and peered into the darkness, then looked into the other small room he used as an office. I felt around on the kitchen table for the matches, and a candle because I wasn't allowed to light the gas lamps if he wasn't there. In the candlelight, I saw he'd left a note on the table. It was one I'd seen before—he had a habit of saving and reusing the notes he left for me.

I've gone for a walk. Go back to bed.

Again, the howl. I stepped into my rain boots, opened the cabin door and started at the creaking; it sounded louder in the night. The half-moon peeped out from behind the dark silhouette of a tree as I walked out to the middle of the clearing.

"Grandpa," I called softly, but there was no answer. The wind picked up, and I shivered in my thin nightgown. The trees began to sway in an unsettling way, and the moonshadow cast by my body looked small and vulnerable. The cabin glowed invitingly, my single candle burning inside. From somewhere up the mountain, the strange call rang out again, hanging in the cool air, and I raced back to the cabin and slipped inside.

That night, I dreamed of my mother. She spoke animatedly to me, but she had a white bandage wrapped around her head and she leaned on crutches, her leg in a cast. She tossed her long red hair and did a little jig for me, and said she'd be dancing again properly by the time the cornfield was dotted green with the first shoots. Fresh blood soaked through the bandage and a sense of foreboding stole over me. I pointed to the blood and asked, with a growing feeling of dread, what had happened to her. *From the accident, of course*, she said, and smiled gently. *Sweetie, you know I didn't survive.*

I woke with a start, my heart pounding. I lay there, tried to push the dream away by calling up the scent of her hair, and the smell of the barn, and the feel of soft, lush grass under my bare feet. But the memories were fading, growing paler, and I didn't know if I was remembering real sensations or just replaying my memories of them. I opened my eyes. Sunlight streamed in through my window; I could hear Grandpa downstairs making tea and breakfast on the big propane stove. I wrote down my dream and hid my diary under my mattress, then dressed and climbed down from the loft.

I was nearly finished my eggs when Grandpa said, "I saw a strange track outside this morning." He wiped up yolk from his plate with a crust of bread.

"It appeared to be a size three rain boot."

I looked down at my plate.

"Don't go wandering around at night, Sandy," he said. "I'd just gone for a walk."

"I was scared," I said. "Did you hear anything strange, last night? Some kind of different *owl*, maybe?"

He stood up and started clearing the table. "I heard the unmistakable snoring of a juvenile *Homo sapiens*. Female, I'd say, perhaps nine years old. Uncommonly loud."

"*You* snore, not me!" I said, "Where did you go?"

He didn't look at me. "I'm making a roast tonight," he said. "Go on out and dig some potatoes."

NEXT TO MY SHOVEL AND a small heap of dirt-encrusted new potatoes, two halves of a worm wriggled on the damp soil. I felt a twinge of guilt, even though it had been an accidental bisection. One half might survive, or neither, or the two pieces might both survive and grow into whole worms and, just maybe, those two new worms might end up *mating* with each other. I was pondering the various complications that might arise from *that* when Grandpa called to me through the window. I scooped up the potatoes and ran inside. I dumped the potatoes into the sink, and told him about the worm. He said that my idea was "intriguing, but statistically unlikely," and that after I'd scrubbed the potatoes I could go out and play with Luke for the rest of the day.

Luke and I were midway through our summer holiday, which I was enjoying even though our "school" was right there, anyway. There'd been some talk of sending us to school in town, but there was the considerable distance we'd have to travel—more than an hour each way, five days a week—and besides that, I had done grade one back in Ontario and hadn't learned a damn thing. The first time Grandpa brought up the topic of school, a month after I'd arrived, I'd told him as much.

"Is that so," Grandpa had said, his tone neutral. I watched him carefully, to see how he would react to the *damn. He* said it all the time, but I'd noticed that was irrelevant to how a word would be received by an adult. "It seems you picked up at least *one* new word that I don't care to hear again."

He'd looked at me, and when I conceded his point with the faintest nod he said, "Very well, you can study with me at home for now. You'll need to be ready for high school in another six or seven years, so we haven't a moment to waste."

I HEARD THE HAMMERING AS soon as I got outside, so instead of heading up along the water-line path to Luke's cabin I ducked under the trailing cedars and stayed on the trail as it descended toward the lake. A bird zipped past me; it was almost like a robin, but with a thick ring of black like a necklace. Not a robin, then: a varied thrush. The hammering grew louder, strong and steady. Luke paid closer attention to Grandpa's lessons than I did, with the consequence that his hammer strokes were firm and effective while mine alternated between wild swings that bruised and blackened my thumb, and tiny inefficient taps that took forever to sink a nail.

When I stepped out onto the beach, Luke was crouched over the railing we'd started yesterday. From the look of it, he'd been up early. The raft was big enough for both of us to stretch out on, but we wanted a proper railing and long paddles to pole ourselves around through the shallows and row out deeper. We worked until we were distracted by hunger, then went to see if Luke's mom, Eva, had anything for us; she tended to have better snacks than Grandpa, who was likely to tell us to go catch a fish or pick some berries. The door was open and the smell of fresh baking wafted out as we climbed the steps into their cabin. Luke called out to her as we came up the steps, because she didn't like to be startled.

"Well, look at this pair of pirates," Eva said, greeting us with a smile. She was hardly taller than me, with the same dark, wavy hair as Luke. Eva had all kinds of nicknames for the two of us, and she would always tell me the reason for them if I asked. Pirates, she said, was because we never seemed to have all of our teeth at the same time.

Luke had already kicked off his shoes and was searching through the small cabin, and I stayed at the door, eyeing the cookies cooling on the racks.

"Mom, do you know where my binoculars are?" he called out from his bedroom.

"I'm sure they're wherever you left them," she said, not unpleasantly, then turned to me. "So, where are you two off to today?"

"Up the mountain," I said. "A *long* way up. Might not be back 'til dinner."

"You'd better take these, then," she said, and wrapped a few cookies in waxed paper. She gently brushed a stray lock of hair from my face as she handed me the parcel, then Luke came out of his room and I turned quickly away and followed him out the door.

THE TEMPERATURE DROPPED PLEASANTLY AS we walked up into the darkness of the forest. The air was damp and fragrant, the forest floor was soft under our feet and the rocky outcrops and huge fallen trees were blanketed in a brilliant green carpet of moss. We followed the trail uphill, looking for interesting things. We hooted to attract barred owls, but none answered. We thought we spotted one and tried to sneak up on it for a closer look, but it turned out to be just a dark fungus on a tree trunk.

Luke knelt down, his face nearly on the ground, and called me over to breathe in the intensely sweet fragrance of the twinflower that was finally blooming. Our jeans were damp from the moss when we stood and continued upslope. The canopy thinned on the ascent, and soon we were scratched and sweaty, climbing deer trails through the old burn with juncos zipping around and squirrels calling out from the well-spaced trees. Luke thought he spotted a shed antler, but it was just a fallen branch. I was certain there was a golden eagle perched on a larch at the crest of a ridge, but when it lifted off it was clearly just a crow. Farther up the mountain, though, a dark opening in the hillside caught my eye. It was at the base of the tumble of rocks beyond the burn; farther than we were allowed to go. The edge of the burn was the limit Grandpa had set for us; so far we'd obeyed him, but it *really* looked like a cave up there. I called over to Luke and he could see it, too.

Luke read my expression. "We aren't allowed, Sandy."

"What harm could it do to just have a quick look?" I reasoned. "And, anyway, he'll never know." I was still stung by Grandpa not telling me what he'd been up to last night.

Luke looked around nervously, as though Grandpa had nothing better to do than silently stalk us up the mountain. I started walking uphill, and after a moment I heard Luke following. It took longer than I expected; as we got closer the forest closed in and we lost sight of it, but we came up over a rise and there it was: an open, cavelike space in the hill of boulders. Soft moss, woven through with prince's pine and twin-flower, covered the rocks and carpeted the ground at the base of the small hill the boulders formed, pressed up against the side of the mountain. We approached, stood at the entrance.

"It could be a bear's den," Luke pointed out.

I shrugged. Luke's timidity always gave me courage. "Well, the bear won't be needing it for a few months yet," I said, and slid between the rocks. "In the meantime, it can be ours."

The space was small, and as my eyes adjusted I could make out the back wall. A tiny spring trickled down one of the rocks and I cupped my hands under it; it smelled mossy and tasted clean. There was a lingering smell in the air, a bit like when a group of elk have just passed through, but sharper and somehow *meatier*. And musky, like skunk currant, or beargrass when it's flowering. Not quite like anything I'd ever smelled before, in fact, and I was beginning to feel uneasy when Luke gasped.

I turned to look. In the soft dirt, right inside the mouth of the shallow cave, there was a footprint. The shape was exactly like my own bare foot would make, but it was twice as big as Grandpa's, bigger than anyone's. My scalp tingled, and the hair on my arms lifted. It was a giant's footprint, halfway up the mountain where we were completely alone and nobody would ever think to look for us.

"Grandpa put it there," I whispered. "To scare us."

Luke was studying the ground. I joined him and we found fragments of similar footprints but there was just the one clear track visible between the moss and the darkness of the cave. I'd stepped right on the edge of it, coming in.

"He probably came over to the cave by walking across the moss," he said, pointing, "Look, see where? Then maybe he lied down *there*, that's why there are no more prints. And then, he stepped out right there."

"What do you mean, *he*?" I asked. "It can't be *real*. Nobody is that big."

I looked at the track again. It certainly looked real. "Or, maybe it's a *she*," I said, uncertainly. There were no *things* in the den, but I was suddenly certain that somebody lived here, somebody who was not quite real in the normal way, and whoever it was might be back at any moment. Luke's eyes were wide as he looked at me, then we scrambled out into the open and ran until we were down past the burn and back under the cedars.

THE NEXT MORNING, I WAS still trying to figure out how to mention the track to Grandpa without revealing where we'd been when he told me he was going for a long walk and I was to stick around with Luke and Eva. He was gone all day, and when I heard his whistle and came running home, he was waiting for me at the edge of the clearing. He was peering up into the treetops, studying something, but he turned when he heard me approach. He was dressed for hiking and his mostly brown hair was mussed, a small twig caught in the silvering strands above his ear.

"Look at this," he said, touching the chewed tip of a branch. "Something was here. Look carefully, and see if you can find a print."

I leaned in. "I see it!" I said. It was just a faint impression on a patch of soft moss, but it had the distinctive ungulate hoof shape. "A deer! A little one, from this year."

"You're absolutely right," he said, but when I looked up he didn't look pleased at all. "You can find out all kinds of things, can't you? If you just pay attention."

My heart sank. He knew. What had he been doing up there, anyway? I tried to shift the subject by gingerly examining my purple, hammered left thumbnail and wincing.

"The two of you," he said, "anyone with eyes could see that you went past the burn, after I'd specifically instructed you not to. Did you ever think, Sandy, that there may have been a very good reason I hadn't allowed you to go up there?"

I studied my shoes. My right toe was starting to push through; they would only last me through the fall. He walked inside, and I followed, hoping that was the end of it.

"You have no *idea*," he said. He turned back toward me and I was startled to see that he was not so much angry as agitated. "You have *no* idea what you've done, going in there."

"Does someone live there?" I asked, subdued, and it was a long while before he answered.

"Yes, someone lives there, sometimes," he said, finally. "Someone extremely important, who may not—" He stopped.

"Sandy," he said, and paused again. The slight tremor in his voice unsettled me, and I waited silently for him to finish.

"You must never speak of it to anyone. I cannot emphasize that enough. Not a word. Not to anyone."

"Who would I tell?" I asked, looking at him askance. "Why can't you—"

"You're not listening. I mean, you must not tell *anyone, ever*."

"Why? Who is it, and how big *are* they, anyway?"

He looked at me for a moment, weighing something.

"We'll discuss this when you're older," he said.

"Discuss what? What are you *talking* about?"

He turned away. "Children can't be asked to keep secrets."

"I'm not a *child*," I said angrily, "and in case you've forgotten, you just asked me to never, *ever*—"

"You most certainly *are* a child," he said. "The discussion is over. And you are not to go beyond this very clearing until I've decided you can be trusted again. For now, you'll stay where I can keep an eye on you. "

THE NEXT DAY I TRIED to pretend nothing had happened, but when I started for the path to the lake Grandpa called me back. I stalked out to the edge of the garden and sat down below the sunflower. Black-capped chickadees flitted above me, pulling seeds and retreating to the edge of the forest to nibble them in safety, chattering happily to each other as they came and went, as freely as they pleased.

I had the common sense of any rural child of nine in that time and place; I could be counted on not to lose track of my surroundings and get lost, not to walk out onto thin ice, or startle a grizzly at close quarters in a huckleberry patch, or any other blatant idiocy. I had always been free to wander far and wide, within generous boundaries, so long as I came home for supper. I knew by then that Luke's absent, dangerous father posed a potential, if unlikely, threat, but even the precautions we took against him finding Luke and Eva here were practical, and limited. This sort of blanket restriction of my freedom was entirely new, and I was furious. *Who* lived up there on the side of the mountain, with not even a candle for company? The only thing for it was to get back to that cave as soon as possible, but how could I do that when I couldn't even leave the clearing? I was still scheming when Luke came bursting through the trees.

"Sandy!" he called out loudly, then he spotted me and veered over. "I found a baby owl and guess what? It was on the ground, maybe it tried to fly and couldn't make it back up, so I picked it up and Sandy! It stayed perfectly calm and just looked at me. And I put it in my shirt and I climbed up and put it back on its branch. It might be still there, come on!"

My chest tightened. If I wasn't trapped in the yard like a chained dog, it could have been me who found it. I imagined it almost weightless in my cupped hands, the softness of its down as it looked at me with large, trusting eyes. Luke was still waiting, his face lit with excitement.

"And you think it's going to *survive* after that?" I asked, calmly.

"It was fine," he said, but his voice was uncertain. "I put it back right where its mother left it."

"She won't take it back," I said, and shrugged. "You should have worn gloves."

"That's not true!" he said, quietly, but I saw the beginnings of tears, and I turned away. I heard Luke running off, but Grandpa came out and called him over. I looked over and saw them talking, heard Grandpa's low, stern tone and Luke's contrite murmur. I'd had it with the both of them. *I* was going to go live in a cave, and take care of myself. Not that one, because then Grandpa would find me, but one just like it. I would hunt ruffed grouse, and catch shimmering little trout from mountain streams and sleep every night on a bed of soft cedar boughs, a fire crackling beside me, the light flickering against the cool stone.

But I couldn't really do any of that, not for more than a few days at a time. I was no better off than a fluffy fledgling owl, crouched on the forest floor, waiting impatiently for its flight feathers to grow in. And yet, somehow my brief presence in the giant's den was potentially catastrophic.

I was nearly grown myself before I really understood the enormity of what we'd done, that even a downy juvenile of a dangerous species, while seeming nearly helpless, carries a scent that announces its lethal potential to a squirrel that is suddenly moved to cry out an alarm, to a lynx slipping quickly across a well-used trail, or to a female primate of an unrecognized and nearly extinct species, returning to her only successful maternity den within a shrinking territory of no more than a few hundred square miles.

FIVE

A FAINT NOISE UP AHEAD, and I find a white-tailed doe next to the line of Charlie's tracks, nibbling on ceanothus at the brushy edge between lake and forest. She lifts her head as I approach, and daintily shits a pile of steaming pellets as I pass by. I follow Charlie's trail as it contours around the edge of the lake, leading me farther from the cabin. I pause, wonder again if I should have left a note in the cabin in case something happens to me out here, though it could easily lie undiscovered for a week before either of my kids would think to come looking. Sam and Lily are in their late twenties, and both have picked up the endearingly annoying habit of periodically cautioning me about safety matters, though at fifty-one I am neither naive nor elderly. I conclude that a note would have been wise, and that, nonetheless, I am not going to take the time to go back and write one now. The trail turns from the lake, heads deeper into the forest. So far, the path has been level and the walking relatively easy, but just ahead the trail starts to climb, following a wide bench until the sightline is lost over a knoll.

SIX

I COULD HEAR GRANDPA CALLING me, but I didn't want to yell back and risk scaring off the bear. I was up in the observatory tower and the black bear eating berries in the mountain ash thirty feet away was exactly at my eye level—a perspective from which, at ten, I was not yet privileged to observe adults of my own species. The bear must have heard Grandpa; it tilted its head and perked its ears, like a dog. He called out again. The bear scrambled down the trunk faster than I would have believed possible, and when it was still eight or nine feet up it dropped. It landed heavily on the ground and tore crashingly off into the trees, then disappeared over a rise as startled birdcalls rang out upslope.

"Coming!" I shouted, and Grandpa whistled back to let me know he'd heard. I scrambled down the ladder and ran lightly down the water-line path, past the smaller footpath that led off to Luke's cabin, up and down the slight rises and dips and into our clearing, where Grandpa waited by the garden.

"Johannsen just called," he said, and I was disappointed to have missed the occasion of a call on the radio phone, the disembodied voice crackling through as though from another planet.

"I'm heading over there now," he said. "Might be a while. He suspects a bowel obstruction."

The Johannsens' goats could eat almost anything, and they did. Grandpa was mostly retired from being a veterinarian, but he rarely said no when somebody called.

"Can I come?" I asked. "I can help." It was a rare opportunity to go somewhere without the hour-long drive to town. At only ten miles away, the Johannsens were our closest neighbours, and besides the goats they had the store, a post office–hardware-grocery combo that had no end of interesting things.

"No, you'll stay and do your schoolwork," he said, already heading down to the truck. "I'll be all day, because I'm picking Jacob up at the train station this afternoon."

Grandpa had told me he'd be coming to visit for a few days but I'd forgotten. Jacob was his only friend who ever came here, and he was taking the train this time, so that he could catch up on paperwork during the four-hour trip down from the town where he lived and worked. The two men had known each other since they were both university students on the coast: they'd lived in the same boarding house for several years but rarely had classes together, as Jacob was headed for law school and Grandpa the veterinary college.

"Go on over," Grandpa said. "They're expecting you."

I had just reached the biggest cedar on the path to Luke's cabin when I remembered my school books, so I ran back home. My novel was beside my bed and my grammar book was on the boot tray. My math book was still missing, but I didn't mind because the search would delay the start of my school day and I needed the time to think about the bear.

It was my second bear sighting of the week, both black bears—though the other one hardly counted because it was just the regular resident at the garbage dump on the edge of town. I'd felt one way watching the bear at the dump and another way entirely while I observed the bear today, and I wanted to figure out why.

Earlier this week, I had wandered around the edge of the open pit while Grandpa was dumping our garbage and talking to the man there. I would have been happy enough to find an old magazine worth reading, or a salvageable piece of crockery that could be used as a flowerpot, but what interested me most were the abandoned refrigerators. Most of them I'd already checked on previous dump runs, and their doors were still wedged open how I'd left them. But I spotted a new one and made haste, thinking of what happened to the missing boy from Toronto a few years before. As I scrambled down to it, dodging assorted refuse, I imagined myself arriving just in time, the strain in my arms as I wrenched open the stuck door, the waft of stale air as I lifted a limp, faintly breathing toddler from inside. I could almost feel the warmth of the child, his small body slowly regaining consciousness in my arms as I carried him back to his weeping, grateful family. It would not be unfair to say that I felt some small degree of disappointment when I pulled open the door of the abandoned fridge and found it empty.

I had observed the dump bear for a while after that but all it did was eat, slowly and without displaying much interest or alertness. The bear I had seen this morning was different; it somehow claimed centre stage, not only due to its size but also to a certain, undefinable quality, a type of effortlessly charismatic presence. I just wanted to watch it, and could have happily observed it all day. But why? Was there something special about bears? Maybe, because it was so important to keep alert around them, the possibility of danger changed something inside your mind, made you feel different, more *awake* somehow? I let myself wonder for a bit, but then remembered I was supposed to be at Luke's.

My math workbook wasn't up in my loft, or in the basket by the couch, or on the bookshelf next to the kitchen table. I noticed Grandpa had made up the bed for Jacob, in the spare room he used as an office, but my book wasn't there, either. I even checked the "bathroom" that was only that: just a tub with the cold-water pipe running in from the spring up the mountain. We didn't have an indoor toilet: the outhouse out back could be a bit nerve-racking to visit at night but I found it, overall, a perfectly civilized arrangement. The big pot that I'd used to heat water for my bath last night was still sitting on the floor next to the tub, and the book of Grandpa's I'd been reading in the bath still lay on the floor. I put the book back on the shelf and replaced the pot on the stove, and decided the math book hunt was futile. I made a quick detour on the way to Luke and Eva's to climb the tower and scan the area to see if the bear had come back, but there was no sign of it so I ran back down the steps.

Their cabin was just a minute off the main path but it was tucked over a knoll, so you wouldn't know it was there until it suddenly appeared, tiny and perfect-looking, like a gingerbread house in a fairy tale. I crossed the small porch in a few steps and pushed the door open, and Luke and Eva looked up and smiled the same smile at me as I stepped inside. My math workbook was there on the table.

"I found this behind the sofa," she said. "I don't imagine you've magically completed your homework without it?"

I sheepishly settled myself in front of my work. It was the middle of September and we'd only been back at "school" for a few weeks. I was still getting used to keeping track of everything, to being constrained by books and projects again.

"Sandy?" Eva smiled to show she wasn't angry. "Did you see the new fairy circle in the yard?"

I had; there was a perfect circle of tiny mushrooms growing right out front of their cabin steps. My mother and I used to point them out to each other whenever they sprang up on the lush lawn of the farmhouse back in Ontario; we'd both lie on the grass to examine them at eye level. I remembered being charmed at the idea of a company of fairies lounging on the elevated round seats, each enjoying a dainty meal of dandelion fluff twirled around a tiny stick like spun sugar, or a single wild strawberry wrapped in a wild rose petal.

"I noticed it," I said. "Very uniform circular formation."

"Indeed," she agreed, smiling again.

While Eva was making lunch, I leaned over to help Luke spell a word and accidentally knocked the huge dictionary off the table. It landed with a tremendous thud and Eva, standing at the stove, gasped and dropped the metal spatula, then jumped back so it wouldn't land on her foot. She snatched it up by the handle and threw it into the sink, then she walked outside without looking at us. Luke and I glanced at each other, but then got back to work. It just happened sometimes. Grandpa said Eva had a kind of shell shock, like soldiers got from the war, only she'd gotten it from being so scared of Luke's dad. Grandpa said it didn't matter who you were scared of, if it was a stranger or someone you knew. It did the same thing to you, made your heartbeat and your sense of safety unsteady, so that either could be jolted out of rhythm too easily. I was not so much sympathetic as intrigued by her rare displays of shell shock, and I couldn't stop glancing over at her when she came back inside. She shook her head and gave a vague, dismissive wave of her hand.

"Alrighty then," she said. "Let's see those fairy tales you've been working on."

Mine was about two kids, a girl and a boy, who lived in a treehouse, and a giant who lived on the top of the mountain. He found the kids and tried to freeze them with his stare, and the girl remembered a warning she'd gotten from a friendly troll and didn't look him in the eye, so she escaped. But the boy couldn't resist; he looked right at the giant and was instantly turned into a toad. I didn't have an ending yet, but was pleased with how it was coming along. Luke said he was done his story and asked if he could read it aloud. I could see that it wasn't anywhere near long enough, but Eva said okay so we sat back and listened.

"Early one morning, I went down to the lake," he read, "and there were fairies flying over the lake, real ones. They were darting and swirling, so I knew they were insect-eaters, so I brought them some gnats and a moth and they came and sat on the beach with me. I caught a fish and there were flying ants in its stomach so I gave them to the fairies too and they thought they were delicious. But the fish had eaten a wasp too, and somehow the wasp was still alive. It stung one of the fairies so she turned *me* into a fish, for revenge. Then, Sandy went fishing and she caught me, but she didn't know it was me, and everybody had me for dinner. The end."

"That's not a fairy tale," I protested.

Luke turned to me, indignant. "*Yours* doesn't even have fairies in it!"

"Alright, you two. That'll be it for today," Eva said, and sent us outside.

THERE WAS STILL NO SIGN of the bear that afternoon, so we climbed down from the observation tower and went fishing. I'd dug up a few worms for bait, and Luke had a selection of lures. He was squeamish about the worms—not about handling them, but about the act of ripping them up and hooking them—so he usually fished with spinners or the old faded spoons we'd scavenged off the beach in town and repainted with Eva's nail polish.

"Luke, did you see that?" I said, pointing up the lake. He jumped up and squinted into the distance, and when he turned back toward me he saw the piece of worm now squirming on the end of his hook.

"Oh, you missed it?" I said. "A mermaid just popped her head up for a second and then made a big splash with her tail. I'm surprised you didn't hear it."

He smiled in thanks, and cast out. I watched him with a mix of envy and admiration. He had a way of doing things that looked effortless and efficient and graceful at the same time.

"Got one," Luke said, and I set my rod down to help him net it. He slid his hands around the silvery little trout. It was hooked neatly through the lip and he slid the barbless hook out.

"Too small," he said, and slipped it back into the water.

"It wasn't *that* small," I said. I got a bigger one and decided to keep it. Luke netted it for me, I clubbed it with a rock and waited for it to stop twitching so I could clean it. It went still and I turned it belly up. I had just pierced the skin with my knife when it wriggled in my hand.

"Ugh!" I said. "Still twitching."

I clubbed it again, then again to be sure. I cleaned it and threw the guts back in the lake. While I was rinsing my hands, I found a sodden dragonfly struggling on the water's surface. I lifted it carefully and set it on my hat to dry off.

Luke caught two keepers, fat little rainbows. The next one I caught was too small. The hook was in deep and when I started to wiggle it out I could see from the bulging eye that I'd hooked it badly.

"Goddammit," I said, and Luke leaned over to watch.

"Right through the back of the eye," he said. I tried to work the hook out carefully, but it was no use. We both looked at the wriggling fish.

"Poor ol' One-Eye," Luke said.

"I think that's 'One-Eye the Fourth'," I said. We only named the fish if their capture or death was particularly significant in some way: depending on the circumstances, it either made me feel like a good provider, or alleviated my guilt at failing to provide our dinner with the clean death it deserved. I grabbed a rock and swiftly smashed its poor little one-eyed head, then sat on a rock feeling alternately guilty and defensive as Luke kept casting. A heron flew over us, a beautiful puppet on invisible strings. We watched as it crossed the length of the lake and disappeared into the wetlands beyond.

Dark clouds were rolling in fast, on a cool wind that rippled the surface of the lake and carried the chill of early autumn. The dragonfly lifted off my hat and flew away, over the lake. We were ready to head back but didn't have anything to carry all our fish back up in, so Luke took off his shirt and wrapped them in it. The air felt charged with the oncoming storm and we were both in high spirits as we climbed back up the path toward the cabins. Halfway up, I shrieked, certain that the bundle had twitched in my arms.

"I bet it's that first one you got!" Luke said. "The one that wouldn't die."

"He Who Will Not Die," I named it.

"Will!" he said. "Ol' Will just can't believe he's dead, poor fella."

We unwrapped the fish and looked at them, but all of them were well and truly dead. The heavy clouds broke open and we ran the rest of the way up to the cabin. We put the fish into the propane refrigerator and retreated to my loft. Luke's shirt was too soaked and fishy to put back on, so I gave him one of my sweaters and we built a fort of pillows and blankets on the floor next to my bed. The rain pelted loudly down against the roof and we counted the seconds between each flash of lightning and the rumble of thunder that followed, until a particularly loud crash of thunder made us scream and collapse into giggles. Through my rain-glazed window we could see the blurry, vivid green world outside. The cabin had grown cold and I was glad to be up in the loft, secretly glad not to be alone.

THE RAIN WAS STILL POUNDING down in the late afternoon; Luke had gone home and I was reading on the sofa. I didn't hear Grandpa's truck pull up, just heavy footsteps on the steps before he and Jacob burst into the cabin. They were laughing as they removed their soaked jackets, both of them quick-moving and agile in a way that made them seem younger than their early sixties. I jumped up to put the kettle on, from both a genuine desire to be helpful and an equally strong wish to be perceived as such.

When they greeted me, the laughter was still on their faces. Jacob was even taller than Grandpa, and his hair was almost all silver with a bit of dark brown. He was of First Nations and European descent, but he didn't know his full heritage because he'd been adopted as an infant, with scant records. The first time I met him, when I had been here just a few months, I shook his proffered hand excitedly and then asked him rather breathlessly if he was really an orphan, like me. Grandpa had spoken sharply to me for my impertinence, but Jacob shushed him. "I didn't start out as an orphan, exactly," he said. "But I think it would be safe to say that I likely am, by now."

He told me, briefly, about the circumstances of his birth. His parents were a teenage couple who'd been, he discerned, rather forcibly separated by the girl's family. There were no names on the birth record: his mother was described as a young and healthy English-Scottish girl, but there was only a single word of description for his birth father. As Jacob put it, "It didn't seem to occur to any of the officials that I might wish to know my paternal heritage. 'Indian' was apparently considered sufficient to encompass the many nations across the province, and I haven't been able to find out anything more about him." He was quiet for a moment. Then Grandpa seemed to be about to speak but Jacob turned back to me. "And as for this fellow," he raised an eyebrow in Grandpa's direction, "we needn't take his advice as to which topics we choose to discuss."

Grandpa protested that he'd merely wished to teach "the child" some basic manners regarding appropriate conversation with a house guest "with whom one has only just become acquainted," but Jacob airily waved off his objection. "Pay him no mind, child," he said to me, and winked. Pay him no mind! I'd been thrilled, and if I often felt somewhat left out by the adult complexity of their conversations, their annoying habit of throwing Latin banter at each other while fishing or playing chess, I enjoyed Jacob's presence and Grandpa's sociable, cheerful mood when he was around. And each night I basked in the rare, cozy pleasure of falling asleep to the sound of adult conversation downstairs.

Now, as we all sat with our cups of tea, Grandpa reported that the Johannsens' gluttonous goat had survived its meal of an apron and a pair of pyjama bottoms. The two men lifted their mugs and toasted the goat's health, then Jacob indicated my book, lying on the sofa.

"I see you've made the friendship of a certain red-haired orphan from Prince Edward Island," he said. I told him that I was almost done the first book, and he said one of his granddaughters had read the series and he was somewhat familiar with the cast of characters.

"My mother had red hair, too," I told him. He just smiled gently, and I remembered that of course he knew that, he had known her. Jacob had walked over to the sofa and picked up my book. He opened it, flipped through a few pages.

"I had sections of this read aloud to me once, when I was in hospital with pneumonia," he said, then lowered his voice. "I always imagined Matthew Cuthbert looking just like Aidan, though of course rather less inclined to talk one's ear off." I laughed, then Grandpa called over and asked if we were enjoying ourselves—no doubt at his expense, as usual. I told them both about the fish we'd caught earlier, and Grandpa told me to run up and invite Luke and Eva to join us for dinner.

While we were eating, Luke told Grandpa and Jacob about the fairy circle and I jumped in to point out that the arrangement of the mushrooms had nothing to do with fairies, which weren't even real—that the circle of small mushrooms formed around the place where a mature mushroom had once stood, because of the spores that fell down from its cap. I looked at Grandpa, expecting an approving nod, but he just looked tired. He told Luke that he'd seen a fairy party there that very morning, and that the lot of them were still out there now, growing tipsy on elderberry wine.

The three adults started talking about one of Jacob's legal cases—though he spent much of his time teaching, he was still a practising lawyer. Their subsequent discussion of the Second Vatican Council was even more opaque, and Luke began stabbing at his piece of fish with his fork, pretending it was trying to jump off his plate.

"This Will is the most persistent fish I've ever eaten in my life," he said quietly, and his next stab at his plate was so convincing that I laughed out loud. I took a bite, then placed my hand on my stomach and turned to him with a surprised look on my face.

"Still twitching!" I said. "Maybe it's a miracle. Maybe Will here is going to be the next saint—or he would be, if he wasn't trapped in my stomach."

"Only one way out from there, Will," Luke said— but too loudly, because Eva glanced sharply over at us.

"That'll do, both of you," she said.

"The rain's stopped," Grandpa said. "Clear the dishes and go on out."

THE SUN WAS LIGHTING UP the clouds to the west, slipping under them on its descent to cast a late-day glow over the rain-washed landscape. The cedars glowed wetly; the forest edge was alive with the joyous calls of hungry birds, coming out to forage after having hunkered down through the long, rainy afternoon.

Luke wanted to look for the giant who lived in the cave, but we'd already looked everywhere. We'd searched up the mountain as far as the burn, and through the forest right to the main road, and all along the lake to the far end where the herons nested. We'd looked early in the morning, when the air was cool and mist hung over the calm surface of the lake, through hot summer afternoons, and at the cusp between day and night when bats emerged from their roosts to swoop over our heads before disappearing into the growing darkness.

"The giant wasn't real," I told Luke. "It was just a smudged bear track. Or, Grandpa made it."

"You can think whatever you want," Luke said. "*I'm* going to look for it."

He set off along the lakeside trail and I stayed there, on the beach. A fish jumped, close to shore, then another. Maybe I'd go get my rod, I thought, do something useful instead of wasting my time on make-believe. But I hesitated. The idea of the giant still tugged faintly at me. Part of me wanted to look for it, to slip comfortably into believing that it was real and that we could find it. I *could* do it. I could squint through the mist and imagine another world layered on top of this one, almost the same, but inhabited with strange and impossible things.

Or, I could just unhook that idea from my mind. I could hold it, shimmering and wriggling in my outstretched hands, and let it go.

SEVEN

THE TRAIL STARTS TO ASCEND the mountain more steeply, and before long I have reached the point where the depth of the snow and the resulting strain on my knees would be better managed with snowshoes and poles. I stop to swing my heavy pack off my back, resting it on my thigh while I unstrap the gear from the outside. This particular action always reminds me of when I was a young mother, taking the kids in and out of the baby backpack, with its exterior frame and blue nylon fabric. Luke brought it home the day after I told him I was pregnant with Sam. I'd known for a few days by that point, and the idea that I was going to be a mother sat uneasily on me. When I saw that backpack and realized what it was for, my first instinct was to hide the thing. For all my efforts to adopt various furred and feathered creatures, I had an orphan's insecurity in my ability to mother one of my own.

. Now, I extend the collapsible poles to the right length and click the locking mechanism into place, impressed by the ingenuity of whoever dreams these things up, and grateful to my daughter, Lily, for the gift. My steps are lighter but more encumbered by the snowshoes, my arms now taking some of the strain as I continue up along Charlie's trail. The trail is steep but not impossibly so; the inclination is somewhere between the generally civilized angle of a deer trail and the steep, uncompromising line of the predators that stalk it. Perhaps Charlie, like humans, shares qualities of both.

EIGHT

A FEW YEARS HAD PASSED since Luke and I found the strange den up the mountain, and with no further sign of the "giant," I had almost stopped thinking about the oversized, human-like footprints we'd seen in the soft dirt. When I thought of them at all, I filed them away with the reindeer tracks I believed I'd seen on the snow-covered front lawn one Christmas morning when I was four or five: images wreathed in the mist of childhood, when reality and make-believe were hidden under identical veiled glasses, endlessly switched back and forth. By the time I learned the truth about Charlie I was just a few months shy of my twelfth birthday, and had distanced myself from such ambiguity.

It was mid-December, and the snow-covered lake was a mess of tracks. Small, leaning marker sticks protruded from the frozen-over, neatly augered holes where we'd been ice fishing for the past few weeks, since the ice had measured thick enough to move around on it safely. I'd only been on my skis a few times that winter, and was enjoying the pleasant stretch in my limbs, the satisfaction of gliding along under my own steam. I had outgrown last year's ski boots so I was wearing an old pair of my mother's, with an extra pair of thick socks to fill them out. With my wool coat, long johns under my pants and my hands swathed in mittens Eva had knitted for me, I was as buffered from the cold as if I had my own furry pelt.

My mind felt a bit fuzzy because I'd stayed up late, eavesdropping on Grandpa and Jacob, then woken early when they left for the train station because Jacob was heading home. They'd been up half the night, talking and playing chess while, unbeknownst to them, I was listening in from my loft.

"So, no luck with that new lead, then?" Grandpa had asked, quietly.

"It didn't pan out," Jacob said. "I met some good people—in fact, I'm planning to go back up there in the summer with a couple of my grandkids. But the dates didn't match." Grandpa's response was quiet, and I couldn't hear what he said next, or Jacob's reply.

After a while I heard footsteps on the wooden floor, one of them pouring a drink.

"And what of your search, Aidan?" Jacob asked. I didn't know what search he referred to, and I strained to listen closer.

"Nothing at all, since we last spoke," Grandpa said, then he lowered his voice and continued briefly. I wondered if they knew that I was trying to listen in, or it may have just been that their game of chess grew more intense because now even their low murmurs were infrequent. After a long stretch of silence, I heard Jacob ask Grandpa if he was waiting for sunrise to make his next move. Grandpa said, "Well, Mr. Kingsley, let's see how this goes," and then Jacob: "Oh, you old bastard."

Now, we skied across the lake without speaking, the silence broken only by the *shush-shush* of our skis on the snow. Grandpa was setting a track easily in the few inches of soft snow atop the old, hard crust. The sky was grey, the lake a bright gleaming white.

A crescendo of chirping greeted us as we reached the halfway point on the lake. A flock of goldfinches swarmed past, rising and falling as one. Their dull winter plumage seemed to me a reflection of the entire landscape: subdued, but somehow more compelling for its starkness. I was watching them disappear into the distance, not looking where I was going, and I bumped into the back of Grandpa's skis when he stopped suddenly in front of me.

"Look!" he said urgently, gesturing with his pole toward the shoreline.

A flash of brown fur stood out against the white backdrop, something cat-sized but low-slung and weaselly. I barely got an instant to observe it and then it was gone—it zipped up a tree and disappeared into the boughs.

"Well, I'll be damned!" Grandpa said, turning to me with a pleased look. "Pine marten! Is that the first one you've seen?"

"I've only seen their tracks before," I said, still watching the tree where it had vanished, hoping it would reappear and knowing it wouldn't.

We continued on across the lake, found the path through the shrubby red-osier dogwood and alder at the back end of the lake and crossed over the frozen pond where herons nested in summer on top of the standing dead trees that loomed overhead. We pushed through another line of brush and back out onto the open flats, then Grandpa stopped. There was a line of tracks at his feet, and I stepped around him to see what they were.

They were enormous. Not hooves, not the round prints of a cat or the ovals of a dog. Raised arches, five toes, the inner toe on each foot larger than the others.

The hair on my scalp and arms stood up and my legs felt suddenly weak. It wasn't that I was afraid, exactly. I felt as though I'd stepped sideways into a dream, or passed through a hidden door into another world, like the children in the Narnia books. The tracks were impossible, and there they were, right in front of us. Grandpa crouched beside the tracks, his expression intent. I took off my skis and crouched down with him. I pulled off my glove and set my bare hand into the imprint, imagined I could feel a hint of warmth left by whoever or whatever had made the tracks. It was the giant: I knew this suddenly and certainly. The giant was real.

A woodpecker hammered on a dead tree somewhere deeper in the forest, and the distant sound only emphasized the eerie quiet around us. There was a bit of a scent in the cold air, a gamey, slightly rank smell, and I felt suddenly afraid. That wasn't the ineffable fragrance of a wisp, a dream; it was the smell of an animal, a real one. I tugged on Grandpa's sleeve. He looked at me, his face oddly alight.

"Stay right here," he said. "I won't be far off, just shout if you see anything—" he hesitated, "unusual."

He left his skis on the snow and followed the line of tracks to the edge of the forest, then went deeper into the trees. After he disappeared from view I waited for what felt like forever, all my senses taut, feeling increasingly exposed out there in the open.

I didn't start crying until I could see him through the trees, tall and solid, walking quickly toward me. He ran over to me then, and I buried my face in the soft, woodsmokey front of his coat while he stroked my hair, told me all was well, he was here, he was here. I calmed down, but he wouldn't answer my questions, and eventually I gave up and followed him home across the lake in silence. Before we reached the beach he told me to go on ahead, to wait for him inside the cabin. Uncharacteristically compliant, I skied back up to the edge of the forest, then pulled off my skis and carried them up the path to the cabin. I leaned them up against the wall of the porch and banged off my boots, then stepped inside, and it was with something like foreboding that I turned and studied the sculpture that stood inside the front door. Charlie towered over me, his body broader and thicker than a man's but upright on his strong legs. Held up by those outlandishly large, very human-like feet.

I WAS STILL SITTING ON the floor when Grandpa opened the door. He looked at me and I saw him about to say something but he stopped, and began unlacing his boots.

"Is it—" I touched the sculpture, paused. "Is Charlie *real*?"

He took a quick intake of breath but didn't answer, just finished with his boots. I kept looking at Charlie, his dignified bearing and solemn countenance. The newspaper periodically ran articles reporting sightings of "Bigfoot," but the accompanying images were cartoonish and silly. There was a statue, too, outside the mining museum, but I couldn't reconcile our Charlie with that giant, grinning ape wielding an oversized pickaxe. Grandpa came and stood in front of Charlie, and I stood up, too, both of us looking up at him.

"Certainly, he exists," he said, finally. "So, yes, he is real. As to whether he is merely a normal animal, well—" He looked at me, and his expression was unguarded, openly uncertain. "All I know is that the one time I stood in his presence, I felt something I have never experienced, before or since. Perhaps you felt something too, just seeing his tracks? Yes?"

He could see on my stunned face that it was true, and he nodded, as though to himself.

"Of course, you understand, Charlie and his kind are not an *ancestor* to humans. And yet, I suspect that his form is so compelling in part because it suggests otherwise, as though an early form of man still walks secretly among us: a close bridge between us and the rest of creation, a relative even closer than the apes." He hastily added, "By *creation*, of course, I refer simply to the whole of—"

He stopped, and shook his head. "I'm sorry, Sandy," he said. "I'm not making sense."

I was still trying to take all of it in.

"Sandy, I need to be absolutely clear that you are never to tell a soul anything that I am about to tell you," he said. "By *soul*, you understand, I mean only—"

He shook his head again. "Put the kettle on, will you?"

I SAT AT THE KITCHEN table across from Grandpa, a steaming pot of tea between us.

"I'd made up my mind to tell you on your seventeenth birthday," he said, frowning as he looked at me, perhaps trying to envision the young woman I would be then rather than the skinny girl in braids and long underwear who sat across from him.

"Is he the *same*?" I asked, gesturing to the statue. "Like the one at the mining museum?"

"He is, I think," Grandpa said. "And, of course, he isn't—not at all. You've heard the line from Baudelaire, about the devil's trick? *La plus belle des ruses*?" I gave him an oblivious look, at which point he apparently remembered he was addressing an eleven-year-old anglophone, and continued.

"It translates roughly as 'the devil's most beautiful trick was to convince the world he does not exist.'" He looked at me to see if I understood and I thought I did, sort of.

"But, why is it a secret?" I asked. "Charlie, I mean?"

"It's a secret because people can't be trusted," he said, and paused, thinking. "A few years before you arrived, a man claimed he'd seen an albino caribou up at the top of the pass, in the midst of a typically pigmented herd. The story got into the newspaper, and within days there were people tramping all through the forest up there, looking for it. Some of them had cameras. And some of them, Sandy, brought guns." He paused again, held my gaze for a moment before he continued. "Of course, many people in these parts are aware of the creatures. But knowing they exist is one thing; knowing where to find one is quite another."

He poured himself some tea and reached over to fill my cup. Hot tea splashed onto the table and I looked up sharply, alarmed to see that his hands were shaking, but when he finally began to speak his voice was steady.

"It was only by chance that I first encountered one of the creatures, myself," he said. "It was early winter, in 1920."

He told me of the day he found Charlie's tracks while out on a contemplative walk and described the moment he came upon Charlie himself. He tried to explain how he had felt, but I already had a sense of what he meant and the words felt as inadequate to me as they did to him. I just stared at him, at the distant smile on his face as he spoke.

"Oh, what a letter I wrote to my confessor!" he said, and shook his head. "I wish I'd thought to keep a copy for myself. Thunderously biblical, as I recall—an irony that wouldn't occur to me until later. The harsh spotlight of truth illuminating the Garden of Eden, my lifelong faith wrestling with my newfound conviction and being defeated as surely and as tremblingly as the angel was overpowered by Jacob. He paused to clarify that of course it was not *our* friend Jacob he referred to, then went on. "There was a lengthy, technical passage in which I thoroughly demonstrated my misunderstanding of Darwin, and showcased an unforgivably poor grasp of the nuances of metaphor in the Old Testament as well. But I made no mention of Charlie himself, and I could see that my confessor, like my peers, believed a young woman must have been involved in my sudden change of heart. I felt strongly that I had to keep the encounter a secret from

everyone. Of course, many have succeeded in recon-
ciling their Catholicism with a modern approach to
science, but I was the sort of young man who lacked
the courage to tolerate any whiff of ambiguity in my
own convictions. I regret none of it, you understand,
but I left both the seminary and the faith very suddenly,
with a string of smouldering bridges in my wake. It
was—" he paused. "It was a rather lonely time."

He told me of finding Charlie's tracks another time,
in the soft mud along the creek, on an early summer
evening when my mother was a child, perfect impres-
sions showing creases on the soles. He followed the
creek in both directions but never found the spot
where Charlie had stepped back onto land, and when
he retraced his steps the tracks he'd spotted were gone,
somehow washed away though the water level hadn't
changed. He told me about discovering the den site,
around the time my mother left home. He'd found
the telltale footprints on the bed of moss that blanketed the area, and retreated to a nearby knoll where
he kept his eyes on the entrance to the cave. There was
no activity, but the next day he returned and saw new
tracks, running alongside a much smaller set, leading
into the small cave. He had waited for the creatures
to emerge, waited for hours and saw nothing. When
darkness fell he finally returned home, then returned
the next day to find more tracks, coming and going.
This kept up for days; he was never able to catch a
glimpse of them, and eventually there were no more
new tracks.

A few years later, he'd heard what sounded like the
high-pitched laughter of a young child, when he was
hiking near the summit of a remote, unnamed peak

in the range to the east of us. He'd searched wildly into the night but found nothing except a few scuffed tracks that looked like the bare footprints of an adult man. And he told me about the pregnant female he'd glimpsed up above the burn a few years ago, after he'd followed her howls up the mountain in the moonlight. For one heart-stopping instant she slipped into sight but she disappeared through the trees within a fraction of a second, so quickly that his eyes could barely register the sight, but there was a flickering imprint in his mind of a towering, hairy shape, a swollen belly, and there were tracks, smaller than the first Charlie's but still massive, leading into the same tumble of boulders where Luke and I had gone. He'd waited outside the den until dawn and then crept over to peer inside, but there was nobody there, nothing there but an empty cave, spring water trickling down the mossy walls.

"And then no sign, for years," he said. "Until today."

Grandpa pushed back his chair. His knees cracked as he stood up to stretch his legs and reheat the tea that had long since gone cold.

ARMED WITH A FRESH POT, Grandpa sat back down. As he talked I began to form an image of him as a young man, studying, working, thinking about Charlie, always Charlie.

He told me that after he left the seminary and was attending university on the coast, memories of the strange creature he had encountered in the mountains surfaced at odd times. A young nurse stood in front of him on the streetcar, and the curve of her hips led him to ponder whether the creature's combination of bipedalism and large head size led to the same issues that often plagued human females in giving birth. The first one he had seen was clearly male—he had been fleetingly, boyishly impressed to note that not only its feet were oversized—but were the females relatively broad-hipped like mature female humans, or narrow-hipped, like the apes? And were the males and females similarly massive? He hadn't gotten a good enough look at the pregnant female, in the dark and from a distance, to know.

There were questions upon questions, and no clear answers. He searched for written documentation of the creature, but what literature he could find on the subject was sparse, restricted almost entirely to newspaper reports of varying credibility. He sought out people whose family history in the area stretched back millennia, and confirmed that the creatures were known across the Pacific Northwest and had existed here before the first Europeans arrived. With further research, he learned of similar creatures reported on the other side of the country, and still others as far away as the Himalayas. Was it possible, he wondered, that Charlie might have cousins scattered across the globe?

HE SPECIALIZED IN LARGE ANIMALS, and became intimately acquainted with the outer and inner workings of cows, horses and pigs. After veterinary school, he set up a travelling practice in the dry, agricultural valleys in the central interior of the province. He was swiftly and happily immersed in the intensity of veterinary work, but the memory of the creature still tugged at him. Eating a sandwich as he drove between farms, he tried to puzzle out the creature's likely diet. A high-powered primate brain combined with such a massive body would surely require high-quality protein. Was the creature omnivorous, enjoying a seasonal repast of berries and salmon and the occasional young ungulate, like the bears? Or, did it hunt or scavenge for most of its calories? He knew nothing at all, and the arid farmland did little to excite his senses or imagination. He grew restless, found his thoughts straying often to those damp forests to the east, across a high and vast mountain range, where he had seen the creature.

"I resisted the pull of this place for a while," Grandpa said, "but you can see for yourself how well that worked out." He stood, picked up the teacups and put them in the sink.

"I'm going for a walk," he said. "You're welcome to join me, if you like?"

I shook my head. He left the cabin, and I sat a moment, thinking. I dragged my chair over to the sculpture. I looked into its eyes, but they just stared straight ahead. I imagined that the wooden Charlie was trying to tell me something, but whether it was to look for him or to leave him alone, I couldn't decide.

NINE

A BURIED BRANCH SNAGS MY snowshoe and I stumble. I catch myself with my poles, and tell myself to focus on what I'm doing before I get myself killed, a feat which—especially since I neglected to tell anyone where I was going—could be handily accomplished by as little as a bad slip in the wrong spot. A memory rises, unbidden, of Luke and I sledding down the steep slope above the laneway, the burning numbness on my face as the fresh snow sprayed up over us, our gleeful shrieks as we flew down the narrow path among the trees and emerged, victorious, out onto the plowed lane. With dusk coming on fast, on our last run Luke failed to navigate a turn and smashed into a mountain ash. Blood poured from his nose, freezing into a bright-red impressionistic splatter on the snow. I haven't thought of that day in years, since my kids were young and themselves tobogganing ill-advised routes.

I look back at the short bit of uphill trail I've covered. The pull of gravity is at odds with my sense of urgency. No doubt, Charlie is moving faster than I am; even if I keep a steady pace, it will take a miracle to catch up with him. And yet, the marks of his passing are undeniable, irresistible. He put one foot *there*, the other *there*. He is out here, somewhere.

TEN

AS THE CHANGE TO MY world sunk in, a disturbing sense of complicity began gnawing at me. I tried to avoid the memory, but I couldn't keep from dwelling on the irrefutable fact that Luke and I had disturbed the den, and that it had been entirely my idea to do so. When it got to be too much I finally confronted my grandfather, telling him I would never forgive him for lying to me, and would never trust him again.

"Considering that you outright disobeyed my direct instruction, it seems a bit of a reach to say that I *lied* to you," he replied to my tirade. "It's not as though you asked outright, or that you had a right to the information; in fact, I don't know that I've any right to it, myself, but I do know and can't pretend otherwise."

"You should have *told* me," I said. "We never would have gone into that den if you hadn't kept it a secret, and now she might *never* come back." I was aiming for a tone of righteousness I'd never before felt entitled to, but my voice broke, and I felt my eyes start to fill with tears. I pushed back my chair, stood up and stormed out of the cabin.

The next day I dug under the snow and made him a bouquet of falsebox and the dead leaves of false

Solomon's seal, with a branch of *Pseudotsuga menziesii* tucked in to show that I could clumsily imply he was a liar in Latin, as well. I left it on the kitchen table, no note, and then hitchhiked to town—such was my subtlety in conveying my disappointment in his behaviour.

I WAS STILL FEELING SLIGHTED a few weeks later when Jacob came to visit. Grandpa had told me that he'd let him in on the secret decades earlier, but I was still taken by surprise when we all sat down to dinner and Grandpa said, "Well, still no sign of our friend up the mountain."

Jacob laughed. "Had you found so much as a single hair," he said, "I'd no doubt have learnt about it in painstaking detail before you'd so much as inquired about my health." It was a bit startling to hear them discussing Charlie so casually—no doubt they had before, many times, but I had never been privy to it.

"I am grateful, Sandy," Jacob nodded to me, "that you and I will now share the dubious honour of being on the receiving end of endless speculation concerning every minute detail of that poor furry fellow's private life. I expect your grandfather explained the reasoning, such as it was, behind his decision to let me in on his secret?"

He hadn't, and I hadn't thought to ask.

"I ignorantly assumed, based on Jacob's ancestry, that he would somehow be an expert on the creatures," Grandpa said. "My presumption was pointed out to me, rather swiftly."

"Neither the first nor the last time I would be presented with an incongruous query regarding the local flora and fauna," Jacob said, "a topic which I have somehow—" he stopped, shook his head. His tone had been light, but trailed off to a weighty tiredness that I couldn't read.

Jacob left a few days later, and Grandpa seemed distant again. He spent long hours at his desk, studying the library books Jacob had brought for him from the university. Now that I was in on the secret of Charlie's presence, he seemed to throw himself even more deeply into his fascination. Occasionally he would share some new piece of information with me, but he didn't notice that I was becoming increasingly impatient with his single-minded focus.

"Would you ever have told me?" I asked him, late one afternoon when he'd been at his desk for hours. I was further incensed that the first look on his face was of bewilderment, as though he'd forgotten I even existed.

This affronted sense of grievance marked my entry into adolescence, and threw a shadow over my relationship with my grandfather. Gradually, though, my outrage faded, or rather it flickered on and off, so that long stretches would pass in which I forgot that I was supposed to be angry. Other times, I hadn't *actually* forgotten but only pretended I had, enjoying a brief respite from my usually diligent practice of being aggrieved. Only when I was raising adolescents myself did it occur to me that, had my grandfather not concealed Charlie's existence from me, I would surely have found something else to be righteously indignant about.

THE FIRST SUMMER I KNEW the truth about Charlie was also the first summer of what would become our annual toadlet rescue. I was normally keen to go along with Grandpa on his weekly town runs, and was preparing to do just that when Luke, swinging an empty bucket, burst into the cabin to tell us about the toadlets trapped in the abandoned bathtub up by the main road. I decided in an instant to stay back from the trip to town, but now my sense of time does a slippery little twist on me, because I seem to remember Grandpa commenting wryly on my "zoological saviour complex"—but that can't be right, that was years later. In any case, when I heard about the bathtub nursery I threw down my book and leaped up to join Luke.

The bathtub had been dumped at the side of the main road sometime the previous winter; we'd considered trying to drag it home but the distance and its weight had so far deterred us. Snowmelt and rain had accumulated as a foot of murky water inside the tub, and there were tadpoles in earlier stages of metamorphosis swimming around in the cloudy water, apparently happily enough; some had stubs of legs, others were still fishlike, flowing-tailed and sinuous. All along the edges, though, thumbnail-sized toadlets attempted to scramble up the slick walls, obeying an impulse to disperse to the higher ground where they would spend most of their lives. I watched one as it gained an inch above the waterline, then two inches, then slipped back in. One intrepid toadlet nearly reached the lip—it was agonizing to watch, I could almost feel its tiny muscles straining—and then it, too, slid unceremoniously back into the water. Another began to climb the sheer wall and I caught it just as it began to slide. It was a pleasant, wet weight in my hand, and I caught another, then another.

Luke and I kept piling the tiny toads into the bucket where they tried to climb the sides, paying no heed to each other's bodies, a squirming mass of slick wet skin. We decided to leave the tadpoles, for now, as they seemed to be doing just fine; there would be fewer predators here than in just about any other amphibian nursery-ground we could think of.

At first, there seemed no end to the climbers, but finally they were all in the bucket except the last one. It sat calmly on my open palm.

"Look at this one," I said. "It wants to stay with me."

"It'll die, if you try to keep it," Luke said, but he leaned in and lightly touched its back. The toadlet didn't move.

"How do *you* know?" I said. "People keep toads for pets all the time." I didn't really know if this was true.

Luke picked up the bucket. "We need to get these out of here before they all escape."

I studied the tiny toad. I could see the movement of each breath under its thin skin, its fragile torso expanding and contracting. Finally, anticipating how guilty I would feel if I kept it and it died, I relinquished it to the company of its peers.

It was probably because neither of us was in a hurry to say goodbye to the toadlets that we proceeded to get into an argument about why a mother would lay her eggs in an abandoned bathtub in the first place. Luke insisted it was a calculated move to reduce predation of her eggs and young.

"Toads can't think like that," I said. "And if they could, wouldn't it also have occurred to her that they'd be trapped when they tried to get out?"

"*She* got out, didn't she?" Luke countered.

We both looked down at the mouldering mass of leaves and algae at the bottom of the bathtub.

"Well, *I* think she did," he said.

We carried the bucket to the edge of the creek, in case some of the toadlets weren't quite ready to migrate, and tipped it out right at the point where the water met the land. The teeming heap of bodies spread out; some lingered in place on the wet mud but the majority began moving up the banks of the creek.

After the excitement of the catch and release, we spent the afternoon swimming and fishing, laughing and arguing and splashing and wrestling. No doubt we talked about Charlie, too; Grandpa had astutely concluded that I would be unable to keep the news completely secret, and so told Luke and Eva in a conversation I would like to have witnessed but did not.

Luke and I ran from the water when we heard Grandpa's truck, each of us wanting to be first to tell him about our adventure with the toadlets. We ran to him, dripping wet, and happily jostled for his attention, competing for the warmth of his praise. We were like twins who, having been inauspiciously separated at birth, had finally met at the age of seven and swiftly resumed their roles as brother and sister. We were rarely apart in those days, and I can't recall why Luke wasn't with us for the second toad-related incident of the summer.

In mid-August, a few weeks after the Great Toadlet Rescue, Grandpa and I were returning from a day of fishing on one of the area's larger lakes. It was late afternoon and the air was warm, and I was pleasantly worn out by the day in the sun, paddling the canoe and fishing and swimming. Everything smelled gorgeous and lush from the previous day's rain after a long drought, and I leaned my head out the open passenger-side window, enjoying the wind against my face as our truck rattled over the gravel. The wind was tugging my braid loose and my hair started flapping in my face, and then Grandpa noticed and told me to sit down properly in my seat. A snowshoe hare ran out onto the road, froze, then raced back, its white feet flashing. I asked Grandpa if he thought Charlie's fur changed colour in winter like a hare, or a weasel.

"No, I think not," he said. "I saw him in winter, and he was coloured much like a grizzly. It would take more than snow-coloured fur to hide a fellow of that stature. There *are* apparently white-furred ones, on the other side of the world—though their relationship, if any, to our Charlie, is not clear. Just before you arrived, I was doing some research up at the university, trying to learn more about the Yeti, which you might know as the 'Abominable Snowman.' I had the most fascinating conversation with a fellow I met in the library, a visiting professor from Edinburgh. He was researching the apparent cultural universality of mythical creatures, in particular those he called animal-human hybrids, in literature and myth. Being unable to reveal my own true purpose I turned the conversation to his, and was able to quite naturally inquire as to whether he'd heard of the reclusive primate said to frequent the Pacific Northwest. He had, of course. He'd initially thought it might be a North American parallel to the European 'Wild Man,' but stopped studying it because he came to believe it was a real creature, rather than a mythical one. Of course, I asked him how he'd drawn this conclusion. He said that the existence of Sasquatches—a name we understand to be the anglicization of a Salish term—had been noted by people from many culturally distinct Indigenous nations, as well as by Japanese grandmothers, an Indo-Canadian fisherman, and an assortment of miners and trappers from a hodgepodge of European backgrounds. This fellow, a Dr. Mackenzie, had no doubt that Charlie was an appropriate subject of zoological, rather than anthropological, inquiry."

"Well, you could hardly expect him to take time away from his important study of, you know, werewolves and centaurs," I said.

"Don't mock the social sciences, Sandy," Grandpa said. "If man is no more interesting a subject of study than grizzly bears, we are surely no *less* interesting, either."

I shrugged, unwilling to commit to a position one way or the other.

"Interesting you should mention werewolves, though," he continued. "The fellow also made the point that, across a broad swath of historical and present cultures, it is believed that some creatures have the ability to change their form, from animal to human, or to and from one of the 'intermediate' or hybrid forms that we often view as strictly mythical. Of course, you will have encountered this yourself, in the works of C.S. Lewis and Tolkien." Grandpa was particularly animated, and it was with a faint twinge that I realized how much he must miss the companionable exchange of knowledge that I imagined was part of his previous academic life.

"This Mackenzie speculated that we carry a genetic memory of our common ancestry with the rest of the animal kingdom," Grandpa went on, "and that this ancient kinship reveals itself in the ubiquity of such mythical creatures. A sort of convergent evolution of the human imagination."

I was confused. "But, Charlie is real," I said.

"Yes," he said. "That does complicate things. I wonder, though, if his theory might nonetheless furnish a partial explanation for my own fascination with the hairy bastard."

He'd been letting more such light profanities slip in my presence, and I basked quietly in the inference: that I was not purely a child anymore. He looked over and smiled, then studied me more closely for a moment.

"You look so much like her," he said, quietly, and turned his gaze back to the road. "She even used to wear her hair the same way, when she was your age."

I instinctively touched my French braid; Eva had done it for me the previous day. Grandpa did this sometimes, mentioned my mother in a way that would seem almost casual if you didn't look closely to see the pain held in the set of his eyes, his forehead. I'd been such a young child when he took me on, devastated by loss and thinking only of myself, and for the first time I began to grasp the fact that he had been, himself, in the depths of a hideous grief. I'd never considered the agonizing four-day train ride he'd taken to get to southeastern Ontario for the funeral; it was as though he had simply appeared, because I so badly needed him. He had walked past the adults, straight over to me. I hadn't seen him in two years but I knew him, tall and sturdy, silver around the beard and temples. He lowered himself to a knee and took me by the shoulders, looked at me. And after days of almost-sleepless shock, my defences crumbled. I leaned into him and collapsed.

After the burial, with all the relatives and neighbours seeking shade under the towering oaks and maples of the small country graveyard, he looked to the assembled adults and said, "The girl will come with me." His hand steady and calming on my shoulder, his voice clear and certain.

I looked at him now, felt I should do or say something, but I didn't know what, and we drove on in silence.

The road passed alongside a small marshy lake where we'd fished a few times. An osprey flew up from the water with a small struggling fish gripped in its talons, and farther on I spotted a kingfisher at rest in a tree at the water's edge. The road was darker here, and there was a brief moment where I noticed the movement on the gravel and hadn't yet interpreted it. I just stared in fascination at the wriggling road. Then the mass of toadlets came into focus.

I was opening the door of the truck even before it was stopped. The ground teemed with tiny toads, and there was a wet flapping sound as they climbed and hopped over each other. They swarmed over my shoes, over the bodies of the ones we'd crushed with the truck. I leaned out and frantically cleared a place to stand, then stepped out. As I set my foot down, I felt something pop under my sneaker. I lifted the lower hem of my shirt and began scooping toadlets up into the pouch but almost as quickly as I gathered them they escaped, toppling back out onto the road. I was wearing only a bathing suit under my T-shirt, and the toads that escaped tumbled over my legs and onto my sneak-ered feet. Grandpa got out of the truck, sliding over to exit through my door; he was right beside me but I saw him as though from a great distance. There were more toads swarming up the bank from the lake every second, and I couldn't take a single step. I screamed and it felt good, so I surrendered to some wild compulsion and let myself grow hysterical. I remember Grandpa talking softly, soothingly, and how I shut my eyes tight as he lifted me back into the truck, and when I opened them again we were miles away.

I was worn out from my hysterics, and disconcerted that I had such a thing in me. It felt new and a bit dis-turbing, and I sat silently for a long time, as we left the wetlands behind and the trees closed in tightly around the road once more. Grandpa glanced over at me occa-sionally, as though he didn't quite recognize me, but there was a resigned quality to his gaze, as though he'd long suspected I was capable of such antics. I was reassured to see that he loved me, nonetheless, almost despite himself. I wondered if my mother had been easier for him, or more difficult, than I was, and to what inevitable degree he had loved her more.

I had heard him talking to Jacob, once, about her. I was still very young, and hadn't been with Grandpa long, and they thought I was asleep while they talked downstairs. They spoke at length about one of Jacob's grandsons, then I heard only the clink of their forks as they finished the apple crisp I'd helped prepare in advance of Jacob's visit.

"She's settling in well," Jacob said.

"Remarkably well, under the circumstances," Grandpa said. His voice caught, and it was a moment before he went on. "It was fortunate, I suppose, that Eva and Luke were around for several months before she arrived. I did wonder about the wisdom of throwing two recently traumatized children together like this, but what was to be done? Eva was in desperate straits, and as it turned out she's been at least as much help to me as I've been to her, what with a young girl to raise and Sandy, well—"

When he continued his voice was strained.

"You know my relationship with my daughter was on shaky ground when she moved away. We were beginning to repair things, but I never dreamed I would lose her so young. Now I feel almost as though I've been given a second chance with Sandy, and I fear that I may not be equal to the task." His voice had been low and now it got even quieter, and I couldn't hear. I had remembered, though, the arguments back when I was five and came with my mother to visit Grandpa at the cabin; the memories were without words, just cold, angry voices. I had hidden my head under my pillow and eventually slept, and for the rest of the visit there was an awkwardness, a tired peace that was not quite comfortable, not quite true. I thought the fighting was to do with my father. I had no memories of him, but I had the impression that Grandpa had disliked him and made no secret of it, even before he, a grown man of twenty-nine, married my eighteen-year-old mother and took her halfway across the country.

I was twelve, now; eighteen seemed quite grown up to me but I knew it wasn't, not really. I watched Grandpa driving, and felt something settle between us, a little. I touched his arm; he looked over and I smiled. We were getting closer to home, and the sun was low in the sky. I slid over on the wide truck seat and leaned against his shoulder, and he slipped an arm around me and drove with one hand. I fell asleep, and didn't wake until he turned off from the main road onto our laneway.

Grandpa stopped the truck at the gate and I jumped out to unlock it, then lock it again behind him. Looking up to the main road, I saw that the bathtub was still there, half under the elderberry and half out, and tilted slightly, like the earth on its axis. I breathed in the scents of cedar and skunk cabbage, and reminded myself to check on the tadpoles in the morning, in case more of them were ready to leave the tub.

Western toads continued to reproduce in the bathtub each year, providing us with annual opportunities to atone for the Drive of Death, as I began calling it, papering over my horrified guilt with adolescent wit. I came to admire the ingenuity of the toads; it wasn't a bad reproductive strategy on their part. Every summer we would keep an eye on the development of the tadpoles and, when they had fully metamorphosed and were struggling to escape the tub, we would scoop them all into a bucket, then tip it out and watch as they righted themselves and began moving upland as though they were one organism, single-minded in its determination to seek higher ground.

ELEVEN

I STOP BESIDE A STANDING dead tree and pull out my thermos and a homemade gingersnap, the last of the ones that Lily and her girlfriend, Michelle, brought me on their last visit—the fact that it is neither burnt nor undercooked suggests that the baker was not my daughter, bless her heart, but her more domestically inclined partner. A few sugary crumbs fall to the ground as I devour the cookie, and I wonder whether they will bring sustenance or some sort of Crisco-induced toxicity to whatever hungry creature happens upon them.

The tree next to me is festooned with vivid yellow-green tufts of wolf lichen, offering just about the only scraps of colour in this stark landscape. I used to pick up bits of the lichen when I was thirteen and had started hiking up the mountain on my own, and was outraged when Grandpa told me that its common name derived from its use as a poison against wolves, for the dubious crime of being wolfish.

And at that thought I feel an irrational but irresistible sense of urgency—as though, should I delay, someone else will get to Charlie first. I pack up my tea and continue up the mountain, my feet heavy inside the snowshoes that are keeping me afloat.

TWELVE

THE SUMMER WHEN I WAS thirteen, I could drive the truck up and down the lane. I could split kindling and keep a nice fire going in the wood stove, I could climb a tree for the apples and then bake a pie. My favourite jeans, though just a bit snug around the hips, were already a good three inches too short. With the onset of my teenage years, I had grown increasingly reluctant to reveal any enthusiasm for the local flora and fauna, flatly refusing to concern myself with whether a particular scratch in the sand had been made by a great blue heron or a wild turkey. I even tried to feign disinterest in Charlie.

One mid-summer morning, Luke and Grandpa were deeply absorbed in their discussion of Charlie's rare nocturnal vocalizations: the precise manner in which the haunting, tremulous calls differed from those of owls or dogs, and whether the calls of the males might differ from those of the females. When they moved on to resume their never-ending debate over whether or not the caloric needs of a primate brain precluded the possibility of true hibernation, I snorted loudly and walked away. I tidied my hair in the truck's side mirror and walked out to the main road so I could hitchhike into town and find a real boy to talk to.

Nobody drove by, and after an hour of waiting I walked back down the lane to visit Eva. I sensed she liked having a girl around, and I would drop in to see her occasionally when Grandpa and Luke weren't there. A few months ago she'd taught me to make a proper pastry, something Grandpa had never mastered, and today she surprised me by pulling out a velvet-lined case full of lipsticks and eyeshadows. I'd made a rather oblique reference to makeup a few weeks back, but didn't realize she'd caught it.

"You know, my sister had hazel eyes like yours," she said. "I think we can find something here to suit you." I'd never seen her wearing makeup, even on her rare trips to town, but now she propped a small mirror on the table in front of us while she lightly dusted her eyelids and cheeks with powder and painted her lips with a tube of red lipstick and a tiny brush. She took her hair down and combed it out, and I watched as she studied herself in the mirror. Her skin, not pale and freckled like mine but a shade she called "olive," seemed to glow and her eyes appeared dramatically larger. Eva's eyes were a rich brown, and while Luke's colouring was mostly like hers, his eyes were a blue she said matched his father's—Luke's father was of Irish descent, like us, and Eva was Sicilian. She studied herself in the mirror for just a moment, then wiped off the makeup and tied her hair back into its customary ponytail. She brushed a stray hair back from my face and looked at me appraisingly.

"Now, these colours are too bold for a girl your age, especially with your fair skin," she said, then dug around in the case and found a sheer lipstick with only a hint of colour. "Really, you don't need any of it yet, but if you want to try something you should keep it subtle." She showed me how to apply the lipstick, a bit of mascara to darken my pale lashes, and the faintest trace of eyeshadow. She did it very precisely and with a light touch, and then sat back and handed me the mirror.

I looked older, and not entirely like myself. I saw that my expression was unfashionably intent, and I lifted my furrowed brows and tried to look more carefree. Eva told me that while any woman could plainly see I was made up, a boy might look twice, see that I looked different but not recognize the artful enhancements I had employed. The air of deception appealed to me and I tried a few mysterious smiles at the mirror.

"You can take these," Eva said as I got up to leave, handing me the makeup she'd used on me. "You're a lovely young girl, Sandy." Nobody had ever said that before and I awkwardly thanked her, then stuffed the makeup in my pockets and ran off to find Grandpa and Luke, to see if they noticed anything different.

I FOUND LUKE AND GRANDPA in mid-conversation—or, more accurately mid-lesson.

"Symbiotic perfection itself," Grandpa was saying, his fingers twining through a strand of drapy brown lichen that hung from a branch. "A lichen is neither strictly a plant nor purely a fungus, but the physical manifestation of the relationship between the two. A fungus provides the physical structure while the algae photosynthesizes, and together they form one organism. Truly extraordinary." He went on to say that the lichen in his hand was from the genus *Bryoria*, pointed out a similar but pale dusty-green *Alectoria*, then leaned down to show us a patch of what looked like tiny living golf tees straining up from the moss.

"From the genus *Cladonia*," he said. "Again, though, I don't know the exact species. Lichens can be tricky to differentiate beyond the level of genus, and I'm sorry to say I've been too focused on other things."

"Bigger, furrier things," Luke murmured, and when Grandpa looked inquiringly at him he just smiled innocently.

"I don't excuse myself so easily," Grandpa said. "Latin nomenclature is indispensable—common names are notoriously unreliable, being subject to regional variation. I recall Lily, Sandy's mother, telling me that the plant we know here as hawkweed is often referred to in the east as 'devil's paintbrush,' and I've occasionally heard our local Steller's jays referred to as 'blue jays,' though that name is more commonly applied to *Cyanocitta cristata*, which are only found east of the Rockies." He reached to the standing dead hemlock next to him, and gently touched the leafy, ridged lichens that covered the length of its trunk.

"And look here! We don't even need to take a single step to find yet another form of lichen. This one is *Lobaria pulmonaria*," Grandpa said. "Does the name make you think of anything?"

When neither of us answered, he continued, "Think *pulmonary*. Can you see how the texture vaguely resembles that of lung tissue?"

Luke and I peered at it, as though trying to connect the dots on a constellation. Grandpa said that people used to believe a plant's properties—shape, colour, texture, in particular—were indicators of which ill-nesses it would heal, and that this concept was known as "the doctrine of signatures."

"Were those the same people who believed the earth was created in seven days, and that dinosaurs never existed?" I asked.

"Oh, I'm afraid you can still find people who believe that," he said, studying me for an extra moment—noticing the makeup, maybe? "It's astonishing how fervently people will defend beliefs that are patently wrong; they will bleed for them, they will die. And yet, have we any right to scorn them? Most of us never question the beliefs we are raised with, yet we are quick to heap disdain on those who arrive at differing views through the very same process. You remember, of course, that people once believed that the earth was fixed in place and the sun revolved around it?"

"Didn't Galileo get into trouble for saying it was the other way around?" Luke turned to face Grandpa.

"That's right," Grandpa said. "He was arrested by the church for espousing what was then called the heliocentric view of the universe. Under threat of torture, he publicly recanted, denying that the earth circled the sun. But it is said that he then, quietly, mur-mured three rebellious words: *Eppur si muove*: And yet it moves.

WE WERE ALL QUIET, IN our own thoughts on the walk home, until Luke said, "I believe in it."

"The heliocentric model of the universe?" Grandpa asked. "I should hope so."

"No—well, yes, obviously, but that's not what I mean," Luke said. "I mean the doctrine of signatures.

It makes sense, in a strange way. I mean, plants were here before people, so maybe we kind of evolved in a way that—" he trailed off. "Well, I don't know *why*, exactly, but that doesn't mean it's not true."

"Now, I wasn't suggesting that you go and start believing in it," Grandpa said hastily.

"It makes no sense whatsoever, Luke," I added.

"*Eppur si muove*," Luke said. He shrugged mysteriously, and he and Grandpa smiled at each other. I walked faster to get ahead of them, thinking back to the way Stellan Johannsen's shirt had stretched tight across his back, and the way he had smiled at me, complicitly.

The previous Saturday I had watched Stellan stocking the shelves in his family's store, noticing his strong forearms as he set down a case of apples and stacked the fruit into a pyramid. He was fifteen, and his body was utterly unlike that of the boys my age. I had noticed his appealing face before, but I had never really noticed anything below the neck—on him, or any other boy for that matter. Now, I could hardly keep from staring. Something about the whole shape of him was suddenly and overwhelmingly compelling.

"Hey, Stellan, trying to rediscover penicillin?" Luke's voice startled me and I quickly averted my gaze as Stellan turned around. Luke was grinning at the older teenager, holding up a loaf of bread with a fuzzy green patch on it.

Stellan smiled and reached out as Luke handed him the loaf. He caught my eye and held my gaze for a moment so brief I might have imagined it, then smiled for just an instant before he turned away. I felt my face heat up and I looked away, and when I looked back a

moment later Stellan had moved along the aisle and
was stocking shelves, whistling. Luke turned to me,
about to speak, and I noticed how young he looked.
He was even wearing an outgrown pair of my jeans,
and I suddenly wanted to distance myself from him. I
turned away, walked over to the apples, lifted one in
my hand as though testing its weight, then set it down
and lifted another, until I felt the flush leaving my face
and I could finally escape.

I WALKED FASTER ALONG THE trail as Luke and
Grandpa went on about Charlie. They could talk all
they liked—I was going to actually do something. I
grabbed my binoculars and notebook from the cabin
and started up the mountain trail. My feigned disdain
for Grandpa's interests served the joint purposes of
disappointing him and putting him off the scent of
what I'd been doing up on the mountain. I followed
the trail until the first plateau, then cut north along
a deer trail toward the wall of moss-covered boulders I'd discovered the previous day; I thought of it
as exactly the sort of place Charlie might frequent,
even a possible den site. I figured that once I found
him—or, even better, *her*—I would quietly observe
its appearance, foraging habits and any other behaviours, making sketches and taking meticulous notes
that I would refrain from sharing with Grandpa. In a
couple of months, I would leave the notebook open
on the kitchen table. He would come upon it and realize what I'd been doing, that I knew more than he
did about "our friend up the mountain." I imagined
a moment of shock, his teacup falling from his hand
as he grasped the significance of what he was seeing,

his subsequent apology for treating me like a child and his ardent requests to be included in my studies, perhaps as my assistant. I was so distracted by the vision of my ultimate triumph that I could easily have stepped into a massive pile of primate shit and failed to notice as I tracked the proof of Charlie's existence across the forest.

A huge fallen cedar in my way brought me back to the present, and I looked around properly. The tumble of green-cloaked boulders looked very much like what I remembered from the den we'd found when we were nine—there was the same sort of damp calm about the place, an inert but somehow powerful presence to the fallen trees and moss-softened granite. A tiny fresh spring trickled silently between two large boulders, and there were a number of spaces large enough to house even someone Charlie's size. Twinflower twined through the moss, pileated woodpeckers had drilled yawning rectangular holes in the standing dead trees and an array of mushrooms flourished in the cool damp: all this was just as it had been at the other den site. I resisted the urge to explore the dark places between the boulders, and instead cut widely around the rockfall to a spot downslope where I could keep an eye on the area from a good distance.

Perhaps I would somehow, fortuitously, come into contact with an orphaned juvenile. The inexplicably but mortally wounded mother, clutching her offspring in her furry arms, would stumble out from a shallow den at any moment. I would slowly approach, signalling my good intentions through hand gestures and gentle reassuring sounds. When I reached her, she would place the infant in my arms; I would look intently into her eyes to communicate my commitment to protecting her child, and after she slumped dead to the ground I would tuck the baby into my shirt and hold it safely against my chest with one hand while I navigated the descent. Grandpa could discreetly find out the correct formula for bottle-feeding an orphaned primate, but I would be its caregiver. I would teach it to forage in the woods, to avoid all humans except us, to take pains to never leave so much as a footprint that would betray its existence. When it reached maturity, we would return to this spot and it would walk away, slowly, hesitating and looking back at me for reassurance as I encouraged it to go off on its own, to find a mate and continue its line.

A downy woodpecker swooped across my line of sight and landed on the tree beside me, startling me from my reverie. There was still no sign of any of the creatures, orphaned or otherwise, and my thoughts turned back to Stellan Johannsen as I continued down the mountain. That night, my dreams were a jumble; various infant mammals clambered on and around me, then my mother appeared briefly, and there was a boy who stepped up close to me and smiled knowingly, both exciting and alarming me. I woke suddenly in the dark and sat up, pulling the blankets around me, thinking about what excuse I could give Grandpa to go to the general store tomorrow.

MID-MORNING, GRANDPA CAME INTO THE cabin as I pulled the pie plate out from under the counter and set it down beside a bowl of apples I'd just picked.

"Need anything at Johannsen's?" I asked. "I'm going to bike down and pick up some lard for the pastry."

"With Luke?" Grandpa asked.

"No, he went home and I just figured it'd be faster without him," I said, too quickly. "Because he's always stopping to look at things, so I just figured." I stopped there.

"Methinks—" he began, then stopped and looked at me closely for a moment.

"Go on, then," he said, with a nod.

I climbed up to my loft and put on my best jeans, the only ones that fit properly. I looked through my dresser until I found a shirt that wasn't ripped or dirty. I examined my reflection in the tiny mirror inside an eyeshadow compact while I applied the makeup Eva had given me, just as she showed me. Then I climbed back down to the main room, preparing an excuse for why I'd changed, but Grandpa didn't look up from his book.

The long bike ride to the store left me too much time to think. What could I possibly say if I saw Stellan? Of course, I would not actually say anything. The thought of speaking to him felt like standing on an exposed cliff, knowing I could jump, knowing I would not. I would, I decided, just smile at him. Knowingly.

Mrs. Johannsen greeted me when I walked into the store. I studied the boxes of lard for a few minutes, but Stellan didn't appear, and then I saw his older brother push his way through the swinging door from the back room with a crate of potatoes in his arms. I felt caught out and my face flushed, hot and impossible to hide. As I paid for the lard, Mrs. Johannsen sent her regards to Grandpa like she always did, but I suspected she knew exactly what I was up to.

A COUPLE OF WEEKS AND two pies later, I saw Stellan Johannsen again. I walked up the three steps to enter the store, by now prepared for disappointment as I pushed open the heavy door, and there he was. He was talking with a girl his age; they stood just a shade closer together than was strictly necessary and wore identical mischievous smiles, their gazes flicking toward each other, then away, then back. I glanced quickly at the front counter. No one was there, I hadn't been seen. I imagined Stellan and the girl swinging their eyes to the door as it closed behind me.

That's that, then, I thought, pedalling away as quickly as I could. Who was I, compared to that girl with her clean yellow sweater and ponytail, her breasts and hips? I was too young—I hadn't seen it before, but now I did. I took my disappointment out on Luke by ignoring him completely for a week until I was too desperately bored and lonely to keep that up.

From then on I was deeply ambivalent about moving any further into this strangely shrunken new world that left me staring restlessly up at the mountains in too-short jeans, and I buried my feelings by searching even more intently for signs of Charlie. One afternoon I was at the edge of the burn when I startled a young buck on the trail. I stopped and stared at him, and after he'd sauntered off I started thinking about the idea of sexual selection. I could understand why female ungulates might prefer the males with the most powerful antlers: growing those antlers and carrying their weight around came with an increased energy cost, and indicated health and vitality and good genes to pass along to her offspring. Or was it only that he could use them to battle for her "hand"? Did she get a choice, or did the males just compete directly against each other, leaving her wishes out of the equation entirely? What if she preferred the defeated male to the victor—could she just choose him instead?

A male robin swooped in front of me and I reflexively nodded a silent hello to it. When I first arrived here at seven years old, I thought male and female robins looked the same until Grandpa pointed out the darker, brick red of the male's breast. What, I wondered now, was *that* all about? It kind of made sense for a female mountain bluebird to be camouflaged as she sits on her nest, and for the males to be so vividly blue all over to show off for those relatively dull-plumaged females, but then what about all those birds where the sexes dressed identically, or the robins, which were so similar as to be barely distinguishable? The more examples I thought of, the more confused I became.

I began walking downslope, out of the sun and back under the trees. I understood just enough to see that, while I might not grasp all its principles, sexual selection clearly had *some* logic to it. When I tried to apply it to my situation, however, I couldn't make any sense of it at all. Why Stellan Johannsen, of all people? Objectively, he had no particular distinguishing characteristics. He was not the biggest, or the strongest, or the smartest, and yet I couldn't seem to stop thinking about him, picturing him, imagining how he'd suddenly smile at me again, whisper confidentially that the yellow-sweatered girl was a bit dim for his liking. I was appalled at myself for wasting so much time on such pointless thoughts, and as if I could escape my idiotic self I broke into a quick downhill jog until I reached the lake trail.

I'd had little first-hand opportunity to observe human couples—I had never even known my father, it had always been just my mother and me—but there was something different about Grandpa when he spoke of his late wife, my grandmother. I hadn't known her, but I recognized the same soft look on his face whenever he spoke of her. Yesterday, Luke had asked Grandpa a question about symbiosis and parasitism. "Ah, now there's a question that makes me think of your grandmother, Rose," Grandpa said, turning to me, and his smile transformed his face. He told us that Rose's mother had to work late each night as a seamstress while raising nine children with little help from her husband, an initially charming ne'er-do-well who couldn't keep a job. Based on her own experience, Rose had declined my grandfather's first proposal of marriage, saying that as far as she could see it, having a husband was more akin to parasitism than symbiosis.

"But, she did marry you," I said.

"Yes," he said with a smile, "but only after I managed to demonstrate, to her satisfaction, that it could be otherwise."

I reached the lake, and Grandpa's smile played itself over in my mind as I stood at the water's edge. The lake was calm. Far from shore, a pair of loons drifted slowly, calling out to each other in what I imagined to be their complex and nuanced language. I turned and took the path along the creek, then climbed up into the forest, a rough idea taking shape. Maybe there would be a function to these irrational feelings if there was any chance of them leading somewhere, but as there was not I was determined to be cured of them. I thought about legitimate plant remedies and unscientific ones that nobody except Luke believed in anymore, and the differences between them, and about how some conditions you might want cured aren't exactly medical but something murkier, less tangible. I thought that, possibly, the cure for my condition might be unconventional as well. I looked at a patch of pathfinder: the leaf shape was almost right, but then I thought of something better and I found a patch of it growing in the shade of a hemlock near the creek: wild ginger. The leaves were sweet-smelling, dark green, slightly fuzzy and almost perfectly heart-shaped.

My jeans strained at the thighs as I crouched to pick a leaf. I touched the soft fuzz on the upper surface and brought the leaf to my face to breathe in the scent. I started home along the well-worn path, with the leaf in my hand and the sky darkening, the cries of crows overhead. My scepticism grew as I approached the cabin. The term *heart-shaped*, as I'd known for years, referred not to the actual morphology of the human heart but to a stylized and not very accurate approximation. And the idea that feelings of love originate in that particular organ was not exactly hard science, either...

I stepped out into the relative brightness of the clearing. Luke was sitting on the porch, working in his sketchbook. I flung the leaf roughly away from me, wiped my hands across my thighs and ran up to meet him.

THIRTEEN

I COME UPON FRESH TRACKS, laid down after Charlie passed by: lynx. The thick fur that warms its oversized feet blurring the imprint of the pads, the tracks similar in shape to a domestic cat's but much larger. No sign of it stopping to investigate as the trails crossed, and it occurs to me that I'm the last living thing in this forest to find out that Charlie is back—if, in fact, he ever left.

Farther along the lynx's path there is a patch of blood, bright against the snow. Stepping off the trail—our trail, I'm beginning to think of it, Charlie's and mine—I find a frantic, zigzagging line of snowshoe hare tracks and a few bits of pure-white fur. I slip off my glove and lift a tuft of the fur, impossibly soft against my fingers. Last spring, I saw a hare crouched perfectly still on an exposed patch of rich-brown earth, seemingly oblivious that its fur was still glaringly white. As I watched it, an insight about safety and illusion had half-formed in my mind but I was too lazy to chase the thought down and sort it out. I could still look back and see it, an obtrusive patch of white, when I was several minutes away.

Now, I open my hand and let the fluff disperse in the wind that is picking up just slightly, gusting so that faint dustings of powder lift off from the heavily laden branches of the subalpine firs that rise up around me. I continue along Charlie's trail but the feel of the fur is still on my hand. I try to remember what happened to the snowshoe hare I shot when I was fourteen, just before our world was breached by the man who would later dwell in my nightmares, whose arrival shifted the trajectory of all our lives. Perhaps it went to the dog. None of us were in any state to notice, by that point.

FOURTEEN

IT WAS SUNNY AND COOL, and the smell of woodsmoke and simmering turkey bones drifted out the open door of Luke's cabin, on that September afternoon in 1966. Our bellies were still full from the previous evening's dinner of roasted wild turkeys as Luke tied their half-grown husky pup, Ross, to his staked chain outside their cabin so he wouldn't follow us. Ross might grow up to be a competent watchdog, but at this point he couldn't even behave on a hunt. Grandpa was in town but Eva was home, keeping an eye on the broth. Luke and I had our .22s, and we went looking for grouse in the brushy deciduous zone on the far side of the creek.

Soon into our hunt, I spotted a snowshoe hare and decided to try for it. A golden-brown alder leaf fell directly onto the hare as I was squinting at it through the scope, and it jumped. Not wanting to lose it, I fired in my usual imprecise but decisive manner, and the hare fell. I ran to it, my heart pounding when I saw that I'd gut-shot it. Its eyes were wild as it lay on its side, trying to pull itself to its feet. I set down my gun and grabbed a rock.

I crouched in front of the twitching hare and put my hand on its chest above the torn-open abdomen to steady it. Luke came over and crouched next to me. I closed my eyes, and for a flickering instant I wanted to just stay crouched there, stroking the downy-soft fur. I opened my eyes and saw the blood seeping over the hare's pale brown fur, its beautiful white feet. I held my breath as I lifted the rock high and smashed its skull.

I should not have taken that shot, and we both knew Luke would've had more restraint. I roughly picked up my kill and stood up, my face flushed with regret. Luke looked away from the small limp body, and said nothing.

I was securing the hare to my pack when we heard an engine running up at the main road. Grandpa wouldn't be back yet, and anyway it wasn't *his* wheezing old truck. I waited for the driver to notice that the gate was padlocked and drive away, but the engine stopped and the gate rattled. There was a logging road seven miles south that hunters sometimes used; occasionally, at this time of year, someone whose beer intake might later affect their aim would mistake our laneway for it.

"I'll tell them," I told Luke. We had several good reasons for not wanting strangers around, and our policy was to politely move them along as quickly as possible. I crossed the creek, scrambled up the bank and trotted up the road, my pack slung over my shoulder.

I heard movement on the gravel and a man walked around the corner from the main road. He wore tailored pants and a button-up shirt, and had an oddly clean-cut look about him.

"Sorry to bother you," he said. "I've come to see my sister, Eva Timmins. There's been a family emergency and I need to talk to her."

My chest tightened. Only a very few trusted friends knew Eva and Luke were here, and I was never allowed to reveal their presence. I realized, too late, that my moment of hesitation had done just that.

When I didn't reply, the man indicated the hare slung over my shoulder and smiled broadly.

"Look at that!" he said admiringly. "Aren't *you* just a wild little thing."

I took a step back. There was something wrong with his gaze, a cold flicker of calculation that was quickly replaced by deliberate friendliness, and it triggered an internal alarm I hadn't known I possessed.

I tried to steady my voice. "You're on the wrong road; this is just the laneway to me and my Grandpa's cabin. Nobody else lives here. You might try the next road south; it's another seven miles, sign says Mattson Road."

"Oh, I don't know about that," he said, looking around. "You don't mind if I just have a little stroll around, do you?"

I stared at him, unsure. He had blue eyes and light-brown hair: it *could* be him. I took a step back, ready to scramble back down the creekbank, but then he tipped an imaginary hat, turned and began walking down the lane toward the cabins, whistling a slow, cheerful tune.

My heart was pounding as I watched him go. I turned to see Luke scrambling up the bank onto the road just behind me, but then he slipped behind a tree so quickly it was as though he hadn't been there.

The man kept walking, and I risked a glance toward where I knew Luke was hiding, watching. He shook his head, gave our signal for "wait": an open hand facing down. The look on his face confirmed my fears.

When the man had turned the corner, Luke climbed back up onto the road. His face was pale and he was trembling.

"He's going to find her," he said, his voice barely a whisper. "I have to go."

We cut off the switchback and headed straight up the steep hill toward Luke's cabin. I was sure the man walking slowly along the road could hear my pounding heart, my breathing that I struggled to keep quiet and even. I was so afraid that I couldn't think, but we had done this many times in play, using the biggest trees for cover as we moved swiftly and silently over the soft forest floor, and that practice served us now.

We could hear the man on the road because he was still whistling, a tune I recognized but couldn't place. We were still a short distance from the clearing when Ross started barking, his chain rattling as he pulled against the stake. Brambles tore into my skin as we wriggled through the raspberry and devil's club that lined the bank below the cabin. We reached the edge of the clearing and Luke touched my arm, holding me back. The cabin door was open and I heard voices inside, but I couldn't make out the words.

We approached the cabin from the side, keeping close to cover and to each other and cradling our guns. The dog was still barking, but he couldn't reach us or the cabin. I stopped Luke with a hand on his arm, jerked my head questioningly toward where Ross howled on his chain. Luke shook his head and I knew he was right, of course: the pup was too young, too unpredictable. We crept up the stairs, moved toward either side of the doorframe. My heart hammered against my ribs and in my mind I screamed for Grandpa to hurry up, tried to will his truck onto the laneway. Keeping low, we peered inside.

Eva was pressed back against the sink and the man stood with his back to the doorway, facing her. Her countenance was flat: I couldn't read anything on her face. If she saw us, she gave no indication. He said something, so softly we couldn't hear. She shook her head, looked away from him and then she did see us, but she slid her gaze across the doorway and back to him smoothly, so as not to give us away.

"Still so beautiful," he said. He reached forward and caressed her cheek and as she flinched I felt cold, as though it was me he'd touched.

Luke shifted almost imperceptibly beside me. I glanced over and he'd pulled his gun around in front of him. He watched his mother's face, the back of his father's head.

"You know I still love you, my sweet girl, my beautiful, beautiful wife," the man said, and his voice broke. "Even after everything you did, I still find it in my heart to forgive you."

Eva tried to shift, move around him, but he stepped closer to block her in. Again she tried to slip past, again he moved, this time pressing her up against the counter. He was still talking quietly, still crying, and I knew the tears were real and somehow that was what scared me most of all. Eva was silent but I could read her eyes, feel the trapped, frantic spinning of her mind.

"We can just start all over," he leaned in and nuzzled her neck, "pretend none of this ever happened. I want you, and you always wanted me too, don't you remember?" He pulled back and looked at her. "Because I do, Eva, I remember."

Her gaze cleared and hardened. "No," she said, and pushed him back, hard. He stumbled, and she started to slip to the side but he lunged forward and grabbed her, and then both his hands were around her neck. She made a choking sound and Luke fired a shot that lifted the hair on the man's head. He let go of her and wheeled around—his cheeks were wet and his eyes red from crying. He looked astonished, touched the top of his head and looked at his hand, as though checking for blood. He laughed, and the sound was jarring, shockingly loud, and he took a step toward Luke.

"There you are, my boy!" he said, arms out. "I've missed you so much!"

"Stop," Luke said, his voice shook but he kept the gun up.

"All grown up, eh?" the man said, quietly. "Well. We'll see about that."

He stepped toward Luke and I felt sick, he was so much bigger than any of us, but then he whirled around and grabbed Eva just as she reached into the cabinet where she kept her rifle. The sound of Luke's gun exploded through the cabin. The man screamed, and staggered as his shot leg buckled. He caught Eva and pulled her down with him. He tried to pin her down but she twisted away, and the instant she was clear, Luke shot again.

A tiny perfect hole appeared in the man's left temple. For a moment it looked painted on, a dot of red lipstick. The blood started and the expression on the man's face was of utter bewilderment as he fell back against the cabin floor.

Eva stepped back, gasping for breath. The man thrashed on the floor, his eyes vacant. Outside, the dog howled and rattled his chain. The smell of turkey broth, still bubbling on the stove, was suddenly overpowering and I felt like I was going to throw up. Eva took a step back, reached again for her rifle. She kept her eyes on the man as she spoke.

"Go outside," she said. We didn't move and she lifted her gaze but she seemed to be looking right through us. Luke hesitated but I turned away, relieved to be told what to do. Ross howled wildly but the sound was muffled by a roaring in my head. I staggered out into the clearing and then felt Luke beside me, both of us staring at the cabin, our guns hanging limply at our sides.

A loud shot rang out from inside the cabin. There was silence, for just an instant, before the echo started bouncing around the mountains, and Ross started barking again and birds flew up from the trees and squirrels called out alarms from the forest all around us. My hands were shaking and it looked so strange, that they were just jittering away with no conscious input from me, and my arms were scratched and bloodied but the sting of the welts was distant, a numb promise of pain rather than the sensation itself. I turned slowly toward Luke, held his gaze for just a moment, then we both turned to Eva as she came out of the cabin—she had a wild, dizzy look on her face and she folded us into her strong arms.

I REMEMBER THE THREE OF us walking over to the main cabin. We took the dog with us and tied him up outside on the porch, but he whined pitifully and the sound was unbearable, so I left Luke and Eva inside and went out and sat with him, stroking him and talking soothingly to him until we both calmed down, somewhat. I don't know how much time passed before we heard Grandpa's truck pull in. Eva made us stay in the cabin while she talked to him in the clearing. They walked over to Luke's cabin, then came back to us. Grandpa tried to call Jacob for advice, though this wasn't the sort of law he dealt in, but he wasn't at home or in his office. Grandpa told us to stay put with Eva and he drove back into town. He returned with the police chief and a constable, and the police truck parked outside looked shocking, out of place. They spent a long time inside Luke's cabin, then talked to each of us separately, then finally left with the body. There had been a photo of Eva, Grandpa told us, in the man's pocket; the constable said a few people indicated he'd been showing it around town.

Grandpa and Eva went to town a few days later and came back with a copy of a report that recorded the death as a hunting accident. Luke and I glanced up sharply when he told us what it said; we hadn't lied to the police, and in any case no one could have honestly drawn that conclusion.

"It's the God-given truth," Grandpa said, and the raw anger in his voice took me by surprise. "And that it took the two of you, yourselves, a woman and a boy, to finally put an end to it—"

He wiped his sleeve across his face, and closed his eyes. Eva stepped forward, touched his arm and then embraced him. She murmured something to him and then walked lightly away, heading to our cabin.

AFTER IT HAPPENED, LUKE AND Eva stayed in our cabin, Luke on the couch and Eva in the spare bedroom. Eva's state alternated between nervously chatty and distantly calm. Luke was pale and quiet, and he looked different, in a way I couldn't put my finger on. Older, resolute. As weeks passed, living in even closer proximity than we were used to, I felt a strange, wild urge to wrestle with him, though we'd stopped that years ago. I was taller, but he had a broader frame. I wanted to test my strength against his, and for the first time I wasn't clear on who I wanted to win. I realized that I felt older, too, and also that a dark anxiety had lifted—from Eva and Luke, especially, but we all felt it. We stopped locking the gate, and Eva took Luke to town and officially changed both their surnames to the one she'd been born with: they were now Eva Maria Russo and Luke Anthony Russo. She bought new clothes for both of them, and got in touch with some old friends on the coast.

During that immediate aftermath, I slept poorly; I would wake frequently, shaken, from some variation on the same nightmare. I was standing up against the sink, Luke's dad was in front of me and he was crying, seemingly out of control, but each time I tried to move past him his eyes would sharpen and he would shift to stop me. I would know what was coming next and try to scream for help but my voice was gone and I couldn't cry out. In time, the dreams changed. In one variation, I glanced out the window and saw a female grizzly outside, and I knew that she was coming to kill the man, and knew also, in the manner of dreams, that she would not harm me. Once I dreamed that it was Grandpa who arrived; in another, the Johannsens' border collie persistently herded the man away and he meekly complied. After a few weeks, those particular dreams stopped plaguing me. Even now, though, if I wake in the night with an irrational terror that someone is in the cabin, it is the face of Luke's father that I imagine, waiting for me in the darkness.

IN MID-OCTOBER, A MONTH OR SO after it happened, Eva gave the husky pup to her hairdresser and packed up the cabin to prepare for their move back to the coast.

The day they were to leave, we loaded the truck, then Luke walked silently down the trail toward the lake. When he didn't return, Eva and I followed. He was standing on the beach, looking out at the water, his hands jammed into the pockets of his jeans. I hung back and let her go to him alone. She stood next to him and lightly set her palm against the middle of his back. He had grown taller than her. Neither of them moved or spoke. It was a cool, clear day and the lake was a perfect mirror reflecting bright-red dogwood and yellow aspen, framed by a dark-green wall of cedar and hemlock. Its surface was rippled here and there: a small trout leaping into the air, the wake of a merganser.

Eva looked at Luke. He kept his gaze on the water, and she turned and walked away, stopping to pick up a smooth stone and slip it into her pocket. Luke was silent behind me as we followed her up the path to the cabin. She wore a bright-blue coat I'd never seen before and impractical footwear. I felt as though she had already left us and was striding along a city street, her brand-new boots clicking smartly against the sidewalk.

Grandpa was waiting beside the truck, and climbed into the driver's seat when he saw us. I slid into the middle. Eva stood next to the passenger door for a moment, waiting for Luke to squeeze in beside me.

Luke stood still, silent, then he sunk to a tight crouch on the dirt, his arms wrapped around his folded knees. We all waited. I wanted to go to him, but something stopped me. It was as though he didn't want to be seen, let alone acknowledged. As though he could just stay there—still, silent, invisible—while everything changed around him.

PART TWO

FIFTEEN

A FLOCK OF PINE SISKINS passes chirpily overhead; the sound carries a long way in the cold air. I break the tip of an icicle from a subalpine fir bough and let the refreshingly flavoured ice melt slowly in my mouth. I'm high up now, and the lake is far below, an expanse of white on the valley bottom.

I unwrap a huckleberry muffin, quickly finish it off and let the wind scatter the crumbs. I stay on Charlie's path up through the trees until, in the middle of a natural clearing, the line of tracks stops. The snow before me is completely unmarked. I think of the time Luke successfully tricked me in a game of "Hunt" by walking carefully backwards in his own tracks, and despite the unlikeliness of Charlie trying such a thing I look more closely at the tracks behind me. Impossible to say, now that I've walked all over them. Surely, though, I would have noticed a new trail shooting off this one. Another thought occurs to me, and I look up. A leap into the trees would have released heaps of snow onto the ground—no such disturbance is evident, and the firs are so tightly cased in snow that concealing something the size of Charlie would be difficult, if not impossible.

I stand in the clearing, my heart pounding, my gaze flitting in every direction. Upslope, there is a change in the unbroken expanse of snow. What it looks like, from here, is something only marginally less impossible than Charlie, but more likely it's just some clumps of snow, blown down from the trees. I set my pack down and leave Charlie's vanishing trail to clomp over. I draw closer, and my first unearthly impression is confirmed. The hair on my arms lifts and I glance quickly around, but there is nothing here. In the middle of this small clearing, the distinctive trail of an adult caribou simply appears, out of nowhere. The evidence before my eyes suggests that the large ungulate dropped from the sky and started walking.

My head spins as I retrieve my pack, pull out my down jacket and put it on. My hands tremble as I pour tea into my thermos cup. I hear Grandpa's voice in my mind, reminding me of the vital distinction between correlation and causation.

I set my pack, harness up, in the snow, and sit on top of it. The warm coat and sweet, hot tea bring my body temperature back up, and my head clears. I talk myself through the breach in my understanding of what is real, what is possible, until I feel more in control. Surely, there is a logical explanation; I just don't know, yet, what it is. The idea that the explanation might be one that *defies* logic sits in my chest, prodding me like a child with a question, but I push it resolutely away.

I have a good visual on the clearing where the line of tracks stopped. I'll wait here until a solution occurs to me, or I have to admit defeat. A small, weak part of my mind serves up an enticing image of my sofa: a book lying on the quilt, a steaming mug of tea at the ready. I push the thought away and take small sips from my thermos cup. I keep my eyes on the small clearing to the north, and let my mind drift and reel backwards.

SIXTEEN

THE CHICKADEE TOUCHED DOWN ON my hand and gripped my little finger. It was almost weightless, its claws a gentle prickle as it took the proffered sunflower seed and flew off. I dug into the seed jar and stretched out my hand again. I was sixteen and almost a month into my summer holidays. After Luke and Eva left, Grandpa and I agreed that I'd go to the high school in town, and the school bus had started to feel like my second home—the ride was well over an hour each way, with all the stops. I'd started my chickadee project in May and it had been a welcome respite from the confusing mixed pleasures and anxieties of high school. Now that school was out, it was a peaceful refuge from the monotonous intensity of my lifeguarding job at the town beach.

Another black-capped swooped in and was about to land when the cabin door creaked open behind me and the bird swerved away, back to shrubby safety.

Grandpa saw what I was doing, stepped back and motioned for me to continue. After a moment, a black-capped landed. Was it the same one? Did they have an invisible lineup, there in the Douglas maples? I could feel Grandpa watching; he'd been condescending about my training program for the past few months but was clearly intrigued, despite himself, now that it had finally paid off.

"Vaguely demeaning, for both parties," he grumbled, but he had the grace to do it quietly.

When the bird had flown off I turned to him. "Be that as it may," I said, "I believe you are *itching* to try it."

He hesitated a moment, then inclined his head in sheepish acknowledgement and gestured for me to hand over the jar of seeds. A chestnut-backed zipped in and landed on his fingers, and his breath caught. His other hand began to lift toward the bird before he stopped himself. I had done the same, my first time, the urge to touch the tiny, composed little creature almost irresistible.

The bird flew off with its seed, and Grandpa was smiling when he turned back to me. "You were correct," he conceded. "A fair exchange, to be sure."

I was inordinately pleased to have swayed him to my position and we took turns, trading off the feeding role every few minutes. Apparently the two of us were interchangeable to the birds; now that they'd decided I was safe, they immediately extrapolated to include my grandfather in that assessment, without any effort on his part. I could have chosen to be affronted but the truth was that, unless one had a missing flight feather or some other mark of distinction, all the chickadees of a species were more or less interchangeable to me as well.

"I had a boreal chickadee come by earlier," I said. "Just one, and it still hasn't come back."

"Is that so?" he asked. "I've never seen one around

the cabin before. I wonder if you're changing their range patterns."

"The chestnut-backed are my favourites," I told him. I felt like a child as I said it, but he shot me a quick glance of acknowledgement.

"The, uh, mountain chickadees are mine," he said, diffidently. "Though perhaps it's just because they are the ones I'm least likely to see."

I realized I'd been monopolizing the seed jar for a while, and it was with some reluctance that I handed it over.

"You know, a very long time ago, I believed that songbirds were the manifestation of God's delight at, well, 'playing God,' if you will," he said. His gaze was soft and admiring as he regarded the bird clutching his ring finger. It looked as though he was speaking to the chickadee, rather than to me, and I smiled when its immediate flight suggested a dissenting position. "I don't mean in the sense of exerting power," he clarified, "but of a creator God, happily engrossed in play."

A black-capped landed on his outstretched fingers, hopped delicately onto his palm to reach the seed he'd placed at his wrist.

Grandpa continued, very quietly. "If this bird is not embodied perfection, whatever could be? Who could doubt the acuteness of this tiny quivering intelligence, the precision of its skeleton? I was certain that the chickadees were among His favourites, as they were mine, and imagined what pleasure He must have taken in gently inking a perfect black cap onto the head of this one, selecting the burnt sienna to daub onto that chestnut-backed." I could *hear* the capitalization of the *He*, a particular emphasis on the word: it was a Catholic tic he had never shaken.

"How would one go about designing a particular songbird?" he went on. "Would one select the colours first, and then compose the melody of its song? What whimsy, what blessed, impractical—" he cut off, and shook his head, then said that of course he had never taken the idea of creation quite so literally as that; it was just something he used to idly daydream about.

I saw the shadow of an old grief steal over his features, and it jarred me into blurting out something flippant: "'That a believer is happier than a sceptic is no more to the point than the fact that a drunken man is happier than a sober one.'" As I quoted Shaw to him, he caught my eye.

"Well. It *was* a pretty dream. And in my case, even *scepticism* is a ship that has long since sailed," he said. "I know very well what I believe in, though I don't presume to claim that I understand more than a chickadee's-worth of its secrets. I count myself most fortunate indeed, Sandy, that at the very moment my belief system deserted me I found another—one no less magnificent, no less worthy of devotional study than the first."

He gazed off into the trees, and I waited for him to give me back my chickadee bait.

IT WAS MY THIRD WEEK of lifeguarding in town, and I'd learned that my new summer job involved disappointingly few opportunities for heroism but ample opportunity to teach young children to swim. I sat up on my perch, my sights trained on a small boy. Perhaps six or seven years old, he gazed out at the water. He'd been my only swimmer for the past fifteen minutes, and he still hadn't made it past the shoreline. I didn't recognize him, and it wasn't yet clear if he was a non-swimmer or just bracing himself to go in farther—this lake was several orders of magnitude larger than ours, so despite its lower elevation it, too, boasted a temperature range that ran from numbingly frigid to merely uncomfortably cold. The floating line of buoys was strung in close to the shoreline; out past the point, the lake was unpredictable.

Several times the boy waded into the shallows then retreated, and just as I was warming up to the idea of providing an impromptu lesson he ran in and did an adequate front crawl out to the buoy line, then back. I was sitting back in my chair, putting on a pretense of not being disappointed, when a gang of kids arrived on foot. They were regulars—two sets of male twins under the age of eight, God help me. Then a harried-looking mother pulled up in one of the rusty sedans favoured by townies, in contrast to the rusty pickups favoured by the rest of us, and dropped off two girls. Within an hour the beach was bustling and I scanned constantly, grateful that most of the kids were waders, rather than divers. Lifeguarding, I had determined, was like particularly attentive birdwatching, if the ducks drifting around and the shorebirds skittering along the water's edge had been illogically vulnerable to drowning.

Two boys pulled up on bikes and ran across the beach, sand kicking up from their feet onto the blankets of the annoyed mothers. The boys ran into the water and swam out just past the buoy line, shrieking gaily as they tried to hold each other under. The smaller one was only about five years old and he looked to be getting the worst of it, so I blew a short whistle blast that was supposed to get their attention. They ignored the whistle. The older boy was laughing, the smaller one coughed and spluttered, then reached for his brother. I felt the scene starting to tilt, I could see what was going to happen as though I'd been waiting for it. I climbed down from my chair and started running. The bigger boy was struggling to support the smaller one and they were low in the water, their heads tilted back for air, and as I ran I blew the whistle again, three sharp blasts, to clear the lake. The other kids came in to shore, and in my peripheral vision I saw the mothers standing up, looking out at the water, hands lifted to their brows. I took long strides against the resistance of the water until it was thigh-deep, then did a modified breaststroke toward the boys, keeping my eyes fixed on their location. They both went under and I felt the impossible disconnect between the place I was and the place I needed to be. My strokes were swift, mechanical, my training an outstretched hand keeping panic at just enough of a distance that I could keep moving.

The older boy surfaced alone, his eyes filled with terror. I dove under and caught the smaller one, his limbs churning and his eyes wide, and hauled him to the surface. He coughed and gasped as I held him up. I shouted at the older boy to swim to shore and saw in his eyes that he would comply.

The smaller boy's body shook and he vomited a mess of water and half-digested food into the lake between us. He couldn't keep himself afloat and I held his gaze, told him he was safe now, I had him and wouldn't let go. I began propelling us both toward the beach in a modified sidestroke. He coughed and shivered violently, his spine and ribs pressed into me and his heart thrummed against my chest. Close to shore I tried to stand up and my legs buckled. Two of the mothers had run out into the shallows and one of them lifted the boy from my arms. The other children crowded around the boy I'd brought to shore. One of the mothers was cradling him. She waved the other children firmly away, and they stepped back reluctantly. The mother holding the boy crooned softly to him, stroked his hair back from his face. His stricken expression suddenly crumbled and he buried his face in her chest, weeping.

My vision suddenly wavered, I felt dizzy and I leaned over, rested my hands on my knees, smelled the boy's vomit caught in my bathing suit, in my hair. I wanted to wash off but all I could do was sink to my knees, my head spinning. Someone approached and crouched beside me, put a hand on my arm, but I didn't look up. Then, a woman's voice spoke gently, as though I might bolt.

"Come on, sweetie," she said, "we'll send the kids away and I'll drive you home."

I turned to look at her and my vision blurred, my throat tightened. I caught her eye for just a moment and part of me wanted to give in, to accept her help and let myself be taken care of.

I stood up. "I still have five more hours," I said, then added, "thank you for the kind offer."

I could hear the stiffness in my voice, felt her studying my face. She glanced to the other mothers who hovered nearby; I knew my authority could be overruled any moment and I would be escorted home like a child. I lifted my head.

"Do you know where they live?" I asked the mother who still held the boy. "He should get checked at the hospital, right away. There could still be water in his lungs."

I couldn't remember whether or not that was true but the assertion of my role worked. She nodded, and I walked into the water, all the children staring as I passed. I rinsed out the vomit that was caught in my hair and swimsuit, squeezing my eyes closed against the hot invasion of tears. I felt myself starting to shake and held myself fiercely rigid until the urge passed. The children still watched me but, crisis passed, they were drawn to the water and they inched closer to the shoreline. I could see the wanting on their faces, the fear that this beach day could be taken away.

I walked back to the beach and climbed up onto my chair. The vantage of my raised perch calmed me. No shorebirds had been lost today. I blew the whistle, one long blast. A moment earlier the children had been waiting with various degrees of patience, but at that moment it was as though they had not known, all along, that the whistle would be blown, and now the sound was a wondrous and unexpected shock. They shrieked joyously and ran into the waves as swiftly as their legs would carry them. They were a school of fish netted and hauled onto shore, then unexpectedly returned to the waves by the hand of fate, or of God.

MRS. JOHANNSEN WAITED AS I lifted my bike from the back of her pickup in front of their store, then we said goodbye and she drove down the long driveway to their house. I'd gotten a ride most of the way home with her, but I always brought my bike so I could ride the last ten miles and she wouldn't have to go out of her way. I was often tired at this point in my day, from being out in the sun and watching the water so intently, but the after-effects of adrenaline had left me in a state of nervous exhaustion. As I rode, I periodically closed my eyes and felt the odd, breezy thrill of hurtling along blind for a few seconds. I was pedalling up the last rise before home when I heard a truck coming up behind me and I moved over to give it more room to pass. After it had disappeared over the hill I heard its horn, a long blast. I crested the rise and it was gone, but a dust cloud hung in the air and there was a crumpled shape on the shoulder, just yards from our laneway. I braked and flung my bike down.

The fawn was small, this year's, and it was still alive. I approached it from behind, to avoid its flailing legs; it struggled to rise, then it stilled, its flanks heaving, a trickle of blood flowing from its mouth. I thought of the pocketknife in my backpack and my heart clenched, not wanting to use it but knowing I might have to.

The deer's fur was warm, its heartbeat slow. Its eyes rolled back, then slowly slid forward, the eyeballs glistening wet and blank, and the next heartbeat didn't come. I blinked back tears. It was meat now, and it would be pointless sentimentality to waste it.

I stashed my bike and backpack inside the gate, then crouched beside the fawn and heaved it awkwardly onto my shoulders. I gripped the sticks of its legs, the soft fur like willow buds in spring, and slowly stood. It weighed more than I'd expected. I shifted it until the weight was comfortable and walked heavily up the laneway, blood seeping into my shirt. I tried to compose my face as I came into the cabin clearing and saw Grandpa there.

"Christ, Sandy!" Grandpa rushed from the garden to relieve me of the fawn.

"Bambi didn't make it across the road," I said. I stretched out my shoulders, tried to smile wryly, matter-of-factly. When I tried to roughly wipe away my tears, I smeared myself in blood.

"Left my bike up there," I said, turned away and ran back up the road. After I'd retrieved my things I went down to the lake, pulled off my bloodied clothes and swam out into the cold, clean water.

If I'd been one minute earlier, I would have scared it off the road and it would be foraging with its mother right now. I wept not only for the deer but for the obvious, if reversed, comparison to myself and my own mother. It was difficult to cry while swimming, and I found that I couldn't maintain the feeling of melancholy, but I was still wound up, and felt strangely fragile as I got out and dried off. I wrapped myself in the towel from my backpack and started up the path toward the cabin, to help Grandpa with the butchering.

The fawn was split open from the sternum, the body cavity already cleaned out. I didn't know why my eyes filled with tears at the sight of it. I'd never killed anything bigger than a hare, myself, but I'd seen Grandpa handling elk before, and once a moose, and I hadn't found it upsetting. I'd always had an affinity for deer; I found their watchful anxiety oddly relatable, but I knew it was more than that. Everything could so easily have gone differently today. Grandpa stepped back from the carcass for a moment.

"That was quick thinking, to save it for the meat," he said. "I—" he hesitated. "You did well, Sandy."

I felt far away, and looked at him helplessly. I was stuck on how they had felt: the little boy trembling in my arms, the fawn soft and heavy on my back. The boy could have died. The fawn could have lived. Or both could have lived, or both died. My heart was bursting with the pain and complication of it, and I felt my face crumble. Grandpa took a step toward me, then looked down at his bloody butchering apron, and hesitated. I shook my head, tried to pull myself together.

"What is it?" he asked softly. The gentleness broke me. I wept against his bloody, gore-stained apron like a child.

When I finally pulled away the new weight was still there, pressing down on my shoulders, and I took a deep breath, stretched myself taller to carry it.

SEVENTEEN

I PUT AWAY MY TEA and stand up. Nothing is going to happen here, and I'm chilled from sitting too long. I can't go back now, but how do I go forward? When all the logical explanations have been eliminated, what is left? I shake my hands to warm them, stamp my feet inside my snowshoes.

There was something I thought of, last night, just before I fell asleep. I knew in the moment that it was important, a potentially life-changing epiphany, but I couldn't drag myself from the edge of sleep to write it down, and it was lost to the night. I am struck with an irrational certainty that if only I could remember, the insight would guide my next steps, lead me through this impasse. It slips around in the recesses of my mind, but I can't get hold of it.

A whiskey jack lifts off from its perch on a sub-alpine fir, circles over me and lands again. What a fool I would look if anyone could see me, now, what I am about to do. Following the caribou trail makes no sense whatsoever. But I take off my down jacket, brush the snow from my pack and stuff the jacket inside. I tighten the straps on my snowshoes, swing my pack onto my back and begin.

EIGHTEEN

I SAW A CARIBOU ON our land only once, and the memory of it is both sharpened and distorted by fever. It was the middle of February, and I had just turned seventeen. I'd been sick with a stomach flu the previous night and had stayed home from school. Grandpa had been away a few days, visiting Jacob and doing research at the university. He wasn't due back until evening, and when he called that morning I'd admitted that I was a bit sick, but told him I was fine, he didn't need to return early. I'd stoked up the fire and slept through the morning in the warm, quiet cabin, and awoken in the afternoon to sunlight streaming through my window. The world outside was muted and bright through the ice and frost on the glass, and though I still felt feverish, the headache and nausea had eased. I shivered and craved something hot to drink. I clambered down from the loft and layered on some cardigans, made myself a cup of tea and slowly sipped it, feeling the warmth spread comfortingly through me. The sun was enticing, and I thought I would go for a walk. It was generally so dark in our forest, especially in the short days of winter, that I was an utter fool for a bit of sun.

I pulled on a jacket, stepped into my boots and opened the cabin door. The light assaulted my eyes; I sneezed and felt a foreboding tremor of nausea. I nearly stepped back inside, but the sunlight sparkled so beautifully on the snow, and the sun would drop below the mountains within the hour. I followed the path to the lake, feeling lightheaded, but rather pleasantly so. Everything looked oddly, intriguingly vivid. I leaned over to examine a pine marten track and when I tried to straighten up a wave of dizziness washed over me. I kept my head down until my vision cleared, then slowly straightened and continued down the path. Before I reached the beach, the nausea struck hard and I bent double and vomited onto the snow. As I started to straighten up there was a ripping pain in my guts. I froze, took a tentative, crouching step and immediately bent double again, then couldn't bear to be on my feet anymore and gingerly lowered myself to the ground. I lay curled on my side on the clean snow, one arm supporting my head and the other cradling my strangely rigid abdomen.

I cried out weakly. I knew Grandpa wasn't home yet because I would've heard the truck, but I was just young enough to hope, against all reason, that he would come when I called. I took a deep breath and the pain in my middle was like a sawblade. I watched the clouds of my breath, felt tears streaming hotly down my chilled cheeks. It seemed to suddenly get much darker, nearly dusk. My head throbbed, and my fingers and toes felt frozen, the skin on my face and legs numb. I knew that I had to get home, but for a moment that knowledge was wrestled down by the desire to be still. I lay there until my head cleared and I realized the danger I was in. Slowly, I tried to stand up but I felt as though my abdomen would tear apart, so I walked hunched over, taking tiny, cautious steps. The cabin was just up the hill, so close that Grandpa could have heard me call out if he was home. He wasn't home. I trembled violently, and the thought that I might be dying was not frightening but resigned, distantly interesting. *So this is what it feels like to die.*

I stopped to lean against a tree, closed my eyes and felt the warmth of its bulk. When I opened my eyes there was a caribou just a few yards from me, its pale fur bright against the darkness of the forest. It was an uncommon sight that I took, at first, to be a feverish apparition, until the delicate clouds of its breath convinced me that it was real.

It took a step toward me, held me in the taut stillness of its assessing gaze. Then, in a gesture that struck me as acutely gracious, it averted its eyes. I felt that it recognized my state, that I was moments from death and therefore of no concern, perhaps even warranting a degree of privacy. I reached out as it passed but I could neither touch it nor step forward, and I lowered my arm. It walked within a yard of where I stood and slowly passed by, lifting its head to nibble at the hanging strands of lichen that provided its meagre winter sustenance.

I stared after it until it disappeared into the trees. My eyes fell on a brown leaf still clinging to a thimbleberry bush; caught in a microsite cross-breeze, it fluttered rapidly back and forth while everything around it was perfectly calm. The effect was hypnotic,

and it was with a great effort that I kept going, hob-
bling the final few minutes to the cabin.

I staggered inside and collapsed on the wood floor,
breathing shallowly. It was dark. I couldn't get up to
light the lamps, and as my eyes adjusted there was the
dim shape of Charlie standing over me, and I thought
how easily he could pick me up, take me to find help.
I lay there, not quite sleeping, and after what felt like
hours I heard the truck, and Grandpa's boots on the
porch. He opened the cabin door and halted. As he
carried me to the truck, I felt a jolt of pain with each
of his steps. I remember the bright lights of the hospital and the sharp smell of antiseptic, a mask was
placed on my face and then I woke, seemingly an
instant later, in a hospital bed with a strange sensation across my lower right abdomen where they'd cut
me open, removed my swollen and infected appendix,
and stitched me back up.

Grandpa arrived just after lunch on the day he
was to finally take me home. He seemed impatient to
have me out of there and was polite but brisk with the
nurses he usually chatted with at length during his
visits. He seemed preoccupied, too, and drove more
quickly than usual; I was still sore and asked him if he
was *trying* to burst my stitches. He slowed down, then,
but I could sense his impatience. It seemed a bit off to
me—wasn't I the one who'd just spent weeks in hospital,
relating every detail of my bodily functions to com-
plete strangers and slowly growing weak on a diet of
chicken broth and lurid bowls of fruity gelatin? I was
still annoyed when we finally parked below the cabin,
and I walked up the path more quickly than was comfortable. He waited until we were inside then made us

a cup of tea, and when he looked at me across the table he was smiling broadly. He looked, I thought snidely, rather demented.

"She's come back," he said, and my initial, irrational thought was *my mother*. I gawked at him, speechless.

He went on. "Sandy, I found tracks yesterday. I was walking up near the old den and I saw that she'd been by it, within a day it had to be. Remember that storm three days ago? It was her, the same one, I'm sure of it, the track measurements, everything: identical. She went in and out of the den, then continued up over the ridge. I had to come back because night was falling, it was too dark under the trees to see where she was going, I hadn't brought a flashlight."

I stared at him. *Charlie?* "But I won't be able to come," I said. "I won't be able to hike." As though that would somehow change what he was telling me.

"I know," he said, his gaze flicking away.

"No," I said. "Just wait, give me a few more days, I can do it."

He shook his head. "Sandy, be reasonable. It could snow any day, and the trail would be lost. We may not get another opportunity."

"*You* be reasonable!" I said. "You shouldn't go alone in this cold."

"You're right, and I'm not planning to," he said, and hesitated. "Sandy—"

"What? Who?" I said, then realized there was only one person it could be. "*Luke?*"

"He arrived this morning," he said.

I was aghast. "Where is he?"

He looked at me for an instant as though I'd asked a foolish question, but quickly replaced his expression with a more patient one. "Out tracking her."

In the swirl of emotions that swept me up, anger was the easiest to isolate. "You didn't want to lose time, picking me up from the hospital," I said.

"I *did* pick you up, the moment Dr. Siebel released you," he said. "And you're right, it's not a task for one person alone. Luke's just scanning the immediate area in case I missed something."

I was furious with the timing as much as with him, and spoke impulsively. "I can see you're terribly disappointed that you had to go and summon your protegé instead of bringing your useless granddaughter."

He looked at me as though I'd gone mad, then the door opened and Luke walked in.

NINETEEN

THE CARIBOU TRAIL TRAVERSES THE hillside, gently ascending. I gain the ridge, and the valley next to ours is spread out before me, the mountains stretching out as far as I can see. The peaks on the far side of the basin stretch up into the lower alpine, much higher than the hills around the cabin. There are no inhabited structures in the entire drainage, just a few decaying trapper cabins, and the absence of human disturbance has made the area a refuge for grizzlies, wolverines, a small and declining herd of caribou. If I were Charlie, I would be going in that direction. And if he goes there I *will* follow, though I feel a tremor of apprehension at the thought of it, the potential for danger starkly revealed by the avalanche paths fingering down from those high peaks.

I follow the lone caribou's trail along the ridge. Just over a small rise I come upon a mess of caribou tracks: they've come up from the neighbouring valley and continue along the ridge in the direction I've been going. The tracks are recent, but I lack the skill to read the whole story. I don't know exactly how many individuals passed by, and I can't be sure if the other caribou were still at the ridge when my stray arrived, or if it just picked up their trail and followed. More to the point, once the tracks merge together I can't pick out the line of the one I've been following, though I remember my grandfather doing such a thing once, measuring all the various prints left by a wolf pack to determine which belonged to the original wolf we'd been following. He did this for no reason other than to teach Luke and me how to do so, and he likely succeeded on one count.

In any case, now that I've stomped all over the trail I can't go back to measure, so I continue following the herd up the ridge. As I ascend, the trees are sparser and there's a bit of wind. I soldier on, sweating and chilled at once. I startle a pair of Clark's nutcrackers as they forage on a whitebark pine; they lift off, releasing tiny showers of snow.

The surface of the fresh snow is thinly wind-crusted, and as I progress it almost promises to support my snowshoe but then gives way. There's a foreboding tugging sensation in my knee as I haul a load of snow back up with each step.

I step into a distinct, massive footprint. Farther up there is another, then another, forming Charlie's particular gait pattern. His trail appears in the midst of the caribou tracks—he walked in the same direction for a dozen yards but then the trails diverge, his continuing up along the wide ridge while the caribou tracks leave the ridge and descend into the valley.

I crouch to examine Charlie's prints, try to gauge whether they're older or fresher than the caribou tracks but it makes no sense. It's as though he simply popped up in their midst and strode along among them; this step underlying that of a caribou's, that one stomped on top of a broad hoofprint. I walk to the point where the tracks diverge and look down the caribou trail until it disappears into the trees, but there's no sign or sound of the animals themselves. I glance around, in the wary manner of one who suspects herself to be the subject of a practical joke. I want to stay here, try to work this out, but it's cold and Charlie is moving. I shift my pack on my back, tighten the straps and follow Charlie's tracks up the ridge as clouds move in to cover the sun.

TWENTY

I HADN'T SEEN LUKE IN more than two years when he
walked into the cabin that night. I remember staring
at him, my heart pounding, a deep grief welling up—
but now, I wonder. I sometimes suspect that memory
is a revisionist historian, that it steals back now to
paint dark shades onto my whole history with Luke.

I just stared at him, the image of this young man
overlaying the memory of the boy I had known, as
though a darkroom error had merged two photographs
into one. His frame was still slim but his shoulders had
broadened; his face had changed, hardened. He was
maybe an inch or two taller than me—I was fairly tall,
for a girl, but he was not, for a boy. He took a step
toward me and offered a tentative smile that I didn't
return. His smile faded and the worried furrowing
of his brow was so familiar, and so unsettling on his
changed face, that I felt my own face grow hot and I
couldn't speak. I stepped past him, my heart pounding, and left the cabin at a fast clip, a faint tugging
pain across my midsection.

I walked slowly down the path, moonlight on the
fresh snow lighting my way, my footsteps the only
sound in the forest. I reached the frozen lake: the

expanse of snow shone and I could see my surroundings clearly. There was the spot where I'd first met
Luke when we were seven; over there was where we'd
built the raft, which was now frozen into the ice near
the creek.

The last day I'd seen Luke, on that crisp fall morning when we were fourteen, I'd woken early to walk
down to the water. Luke was already there, fishing
off the anchored raft far out in the lake, the canoe
bobbing on its rope amid the reflections of the trees
reaching in toward him. He was casting out in the
direction of the far shore and didn't see me. I was
about to call to him, but I'd never looked at him from
such a distance and a sudden shyness held me back. I
turned to leave. Just as I reached the edge of the trees,
he called my name. His voice rang out clearly across
the water, but I didn't turn back.

Now I shivered in the cold night, and wrapped my
arms around myself for warmth. I was both excited
about Charlie and taken aback by my confusion over
Luke's arrival, and wanted time to think before I
returned to the cabin. The placement of my incision
made it impossible to wear pants, and under my sweaters I wore a thin and moth-eaten wool dress—it was
the only one I had, and it offered little protection from
the cold. I blew on my hands to warm them, looked
at the glow of the cabin through the trees. I climbed
the path, crossed the clearing and climbed the steps. A
narrow band of snow rested precariously on the porch
rail, and I nudged it off. I stood a moment before the
door, then opened it and stepped inside.

Luke and Grandpa were sitting by the fire, talking
intently. I pulled off my boots and sat down at the

table. Luke glanced over at me, but then Grandpa asked him a question and he looked down, thinking.

"No," he said. "Nothing else, but what does that—"

"I don't know," Grandpa said, and closed his eyes for a moment. He looked old and defeated, and I felt ashamed of my obnoxious behaviour earlier.

Then he stood up. "We'll go out at first light," he said to Luke, who nodded. Then Grandpa looked at me, a flicker of a glance back toward Luke, and said he would be right back. The cabin door closed behind him, and Luke came and sat with me at the table.

"I lost the trail," he said, as though it was perfectly natural that he would be here, talking to me. "It just stopped."

I squinted at him, disconcerted. I'd been thinking about him as much as Charlie, but felt compelled to answer intelligently.

"How could it just *stop*?" I asked. "That doesn't make sense. Did you check all the trees?"

He shook his head. "I looked everywhere," he said. "It doesn't make sense."

"Did you ever think—" I began, but stopped when he caught my eye and smiled, stood up and mimed stepping backwards in his own tracks.

"She would have backed right into me," he said, and sat back down. "Or else she would have had to cut off, somewhere. I would've seen the tracks. That's what I don't understand. Tracks can't be *wrong*."

He looked away, then, and stared into the fire. I could feel him thinking, trying to puzzle it out. I turned my gaze toward the fire too, but my eyes kept flicking back to watch him. The dark stubble on his jaw accentuated the deep blue of his eyes. His arm rested casually on the table and his sleeve was pushed up, his forearm strong with new muscle. He glanced over, met my eyes a moment, smiled before I looked quickly away. He was Luke, but I didn't know him anymore. A stranger.

I SLEPT POORLY, DISTRACTED BY the prospect of Charlie out there, of Luke sleeping downstairs on the sofa. He and Grandpa rose when the sky was just starting to brighten, and I heard them whispering to each other so as not to wake me. I waited until they were gone before climbing down from the loft, noticing my incision was marginally less tender. If Charlie had seen fit to pass through just a few weeks later, I might have been up for the mission. A few weeks earlier, and Grandpa might have had to carry me out of the mountains. I might have even died. The thought made me feel oddly important; it was satisfying to think myself capable of something so conclusive, so dramatic as dying of a burst appendix.

Luke's backpack lay on the floor beside the sofa. I was curious about its contents but couldn't countenance the indignity of snooping. I ate breakfast, tracked Luke and Grandpa down to the lake and partway around it, then turned back—they'd soon discover how far I'd gone, and Grandpa had told me I needed to rest. When I entered the cabin my eyes were drawn, again, to Luke's pack. I carefully opened it, took out a pair of jeans and a novel by a man with a German name. I found a faded T-shirt, soft and well-worn. I held it to my face, breathed in for just an instant, then hastily repacked the bag. I returned to the couch, and to my homework.

IN MID-AFTERNOON I MADE SOME soup, enjoying the distraction. I waited until dark, then finally helped myself to a bowl and was nearly finished when I heard them banging their boots on the porch.

I opened the door before they could and they both looked at me, startled. Their cheeks were reddened with cold, and the hair straying from under their hats was so frosted that Luke's was as white as Grandpa's. As they stepped inside, they caught each other's eyes and I felt Grandpa offer Luke something, and Luke defer to Grandpa.

"Sandy," Grandpa said, "it wasn't just the one. She's got a juvenile with her, she'd have been carrying it earlier so we didn't know, but we found the place where she let it down. Both their tracks, one after the other. The juvenile weighed very little, I think, perhaps fifteen or twenty pounds, and its feet were small—well, relatively large, of course, but no bigger than those of a five-year-old child. It was the strangest thing, the size of the tracks holding up something so light: as though you'd crossed a human child with a snowshoe hare."

I stared at him in disbelief when he paused. *And*?

"Then both sets of tracks just stopped," he said. "Just—nothing."

TWENTY-ONE

A FEW SNOWFLAKES FALL, BUT I'm deep in thought and hardly register them. Grandpa asked me something, not long after he and Luke followed Charlie's trail. Grandpa had come out of his office, into the main room of the cabin. He'd been staying up late for the previous several days, trying to work something out, and he looked exhausted.

He asked me, "Are you familiar with the term *transubstantiation*?" I wasn't, and he started to explain. "It's the process of bread becoming the body of Christ, the wine becoming His blood, in the Holy Eucharist." His eyes were distant; I could almost see his mind working, but I couldn't follow where he was headed.

"You mean, literally?" I asked, wrinkling my nose.

"I was just thinking," he said, "about Charlie, and what happened with the tracks." He stopped, shook his head. "Never mind. I had an idea, but it can't be right. I fear my early acquaintance with mysticism is now clouding my thoughts. One can leave a religion, to be sure, but there are phantom pains. Fragments linger, of both shrapnel and magic, and forever after there is the chance, the risk, that either can make its way to one's heart."

He'd stopped then, looked at me, took in my bemused expression. "Forgive me, Sandy," he said. "An old man's ramblings, nothing more." He returned to his office and sat at his desk, resting his head in his hands.

He didn't say anything about such risks being hereditary, but now I wonder. I examine the sky, trying to assess whether these first falling flakes are just strays, or harbingers of a storm. The wind is light, the clouds are thin and high above me, but to the west the sky is darker and will need watching. With this change in weather, the veneer of prettiness and enchantment is stripped from the landscape to reveal the stark, mortal beauty of winter mountains. A single snowflake lands on my glove, its gorgeous crystalline structure intact, and I admire it for a moment, then blow it lightly away. I feel how easily my intention could turn weightless and simply float off in the light breeze, how it would seem almost blameless.

My fingers and toes are chilled, my back sweaty beneath my pack. A light gust lifts fresh snow from the ground and trees, and I am briefly enveloped in a fine mist of powder. I keep walking. My legs ache with each step; "walking" is hardly the right word for what it takes for a human, even with the help of snowshoes, to move uphill through snow. Sam recently told me how many calories are burned doing this—one thousand an hour? Something outrageous. Explaining why he was able to put back a third plate of lasagne after a day of ski guiding—my son, broad-shouldered and strong from physical work but spare and lean. More or less the size his father was, though Sam, at almost thirty, is already several years older than I ever saw

Luke. Tiny lines now set up permanently at the out-side edges of my son's blue eyes, faint vertical creases scored into his forehead.

The ridge broadens as it curves to the west, level-ling out to gentle dips and rises. There are more tracks: squirrels, a snowshoe hare, a pine marten. Charlie's trail is straight, unwavering and lightly dusted with fresh snow. The tracks skirt a burnt-out ponderosa pine, its blackened trunk garlanded with wolf lichen.

I come up over a small rise and the trail ahead of me doesn't look right. I rush forward until I am standing in Charlie's footprint with no next step laid out in front of me. I can see the spot far up the ridge where he took his next step but the space between them is surely impossible, even for Charlie. A pine marten trail links the two prints, leaving marks from the countless small steps it took to bridge the distance.

I walk over to confirm that the track up ahead is Charlie's left foot, then walk back, roughly measuring the distance between his steps. The space is ten yards, maybe more, and there's no change in his gait pattern leading up to it. I think about Olympian long-jumpers, about monkeys swinging between trees and cheetahs almost flying as they go for a kill, and still I stare at the space in the snow, baffled. There's a visible start and finish point to the marten's trail, its tracks appear just beyond the huge footprint at my feet and stop ten yards away, where Charlie's pick up the trail.

It occurs to me that Charlie is playing games with me. My daughter, Lily, told me about a time she was doing winter fieldwork, tracking a particularly elusive male cougar as snow fell and dusk approached. She finally had to stop for the day, and when she'd hiked back to her snowmobile she found the cat's huge, fresh tracks all around it, a haughty spray of piss letting her know what he thought of her research.

A squirrel calls out an alarm, and I flinch. I skirt around the pine marten tracks to rejoin Charlie's trail and continue along the ridge, watching the sky and fighting the urge to glance back over my shoulder with each step.

TWENTY-TWO

I'D BEEN DISTRACTED SINCE LUKE returned to the coast to finish his last year of high school. He'd stayed with us for three days; it was just long enough for the memories of us together as children to come flooding back, but not long enough to really reconcile that with the way it felt to be near him now.

The evening before he left, Grandpa went out for a moonlit stroll and Luke and I sat together on the couch. He was sketching Charlie's footprints and I was pretending to read my book, but I felt too awkward, too intrigued by his proximity to focus on the pages. I briefly tried to pull myself together; then, emboldened by the firelight and the late hour, I set my book down on the couch. I didn't say anything, but he set his notebook down and looked over at me, and we caught each other's eyes. For just a moment he was the old Luke, but almost immediately he was a stranger again. He reached forward, brushed back a loose strand of my hair so lightly that my breath caught.

"Well," he said, quietly, "Cassandra Langley."

He held my gaze and I didn't look away.

I set my hand lightly on his leg, then felt so overwhelmed that I closed my eyes. Luke moved closer and slid his arm around me and I let my head rest against his shoulder and I wanted to just stay there for as long as it took for the lost years to catch up and spill into each other.

Grandpa banged his boots loudly on the porch outside, and I slipped away from Luke and stood up. When Grandpa came inside, Luke was on the couch, sketching in his notebook, and I was standing in front of the bookshelf, apparently engrossed in selecting some reading material. For a moment Grandpa looked appraisingly at us, at my open book lying on the couch, then he lit a burner and put the kettle on.

In the morning, I hung back as Luke and Grandpa said their goodbyes at the train station, their heads close together and voices lowered. Then Luke walked over to me, his countenance determined, as though steeling himself. He stood in front of me, held my gaze as he reached forward and took my hand in both of his.

"Sandy," he said, and then looked down, a flurry of emotion on his face.

I wanted to say, *You don't have to go. You can stay, finish grade twelve here. With me.* But my courage failed.

I said, "I'm glad you came back. To help, I mean." I couldn't think of anything else to say; I should have thought about it earlier. He released my hand, leaned in and swiftly kissed my cheek. His smile was startlingly unguarded, for just an instant, then he composed himself, turned and bounded onto the train.

WHEN GRANDPA GLANCED AT THE letter addressed to Luke, I quickly said that I'd promised to keep him posted on our search for Charlie. I'd waited for two weeks after he left but could contain myself no longer. No doubt Grandpa saw right through me, but I was grateful that he gave no indication. I'd tried to write to Luke about what I was feeling, to tell him that every-thing had changed in the brief time he'd been here. That I could still feel the warmth of his arm around me, the intensity of his gaze at the train station. That my world had tilted just slightly on its axis and I couldn't go on as though nothing had changed. I'd lost my bearings and was circling, trying to get back to that place where everything made sense.

That letter went straight into the fire—not the paper bin but directly into the stove, furtively, while Grandpa was out walking. Instead, I wrote to Luke about the sudden absence of the whiskey jack that normally greeted us each morning when we came out of the cabin. I wrote that ice fishing was just about done for the season, and as the days grew longer I wasn't able to keep such a close eye on the stars and was worried that certain constellations were being lost to us. What if they never reappeared? I asked him if he even remembered what stars look like, as he was no doubt night-blind from all the lights in the city.

He wrote back that his eyes were starved for the particular green of the cedars around our cabin, that the ocean was wild and beautiful to look at but he craved a frozen river or lake, something to skate on. His handwriting was small and messy, and his letter had small sketches scattered throughout, of his room in the apartment building where he lived with his mother, of the rock doves and crows and songbirds he watched through the windows during his classes at the huge high school he attended.

I wrote again and told him about the pair of goldeneyes I'd seen circling in a bathtub-sized patch of open water on the otherwise-frozen lake. I sent him a fragrant sprig of grand fir, telling him that the contrast between the dark-green needles and the fresh pale-green tips reminded me of the two-toned gloves his mother used to knit for us when we were small. The bulky envelope he sent in reply included a greeting from Eva and a pair of gloves she'd made for me, dark green with pale green fingertips. He wrote that he'd spotted Charlie on a streetcar the previous Tuesday; he'd tried to follow but Charlie lost him in the crowd. I wrote back that, coincidentally, I had spent an engaging afternoon with Charlie that very same Tuesday; she'd cajoled me into putting extra raisins in the bran muffins, and had taken her tea black, with sugar. I wrote that Charlie sent her warmest greetings to Luke and Eva, and had asked me to kindly relay the message that she was nearly finished knitting them a tea cozy as a belated housewarming gift.

Perhaps we should introduce the two Charlies, he wrote, encourage them to reproduce and continue their line. He wrote that the mass of people living in the city reminded him of tangling vines on a stone building—unable to stand alone, always clinging to some structure or another. He wrote to me from English class, told me his teacher was going on about Kafka but he wasn't listening; he was looking out the window and wishing he would wake up one morning as a song sparrow. He sent me an elaborate hand-drawn map of the mountain ranges and river valleys between us, and, once, with no attached letter and no explanation, an ancient-looking key.

I wrote to him about a female merganser I'd seen—she reminded me of an overloaded canoe, barely able to keep afloat under the weight of nine squirming ducklings on her back—and I told him about the baby sandpiper that ran across the beach looking just like a cotton ball with toothpicks for legs. I asked him what he was doing this summer, told him he could come and visit us, if he wanted to. I tucked the letter into the envelope, slipped in three dried morels and a single cottonwood bud, fragrant with thick red resin.

We both finished high school. I returned to my life-guarding job in town, and he got a construction job in the city. *Just for a month or so*, he wrote. *I'll be there before the raspberries are ripe. There are too many people living in this building, in this damn city. I don't want to get tangled up in all these vines.*

I told him that the shrubby side of the creek was thick with snowshoe hares, and the baby osprey were in their nest above the rockfall, loudly harassing their parents for fish. I told him the fishing was excellent, and what was taking him so long? How many houses did these city people *need*? And if cities were so terrible, why did so many people live in them?

To that last, he wrote in reply: *Stockholm Syndrome, obviously.* That didn't make sense, exactly, but for some reason it pleased me. Luke's irrational streak had often irritated me when we were children, but now it gave off the alluring shimmer of the illicit.

One afternoon I was grouse hunting across the creek when a spot of red caught my eye and I reached carefully into a tangle of branches to pluck a single raspberry, perfectly ripe. I wrote to Luke that if he thought I was just going to wait around until huckle-berry season he had another think coming. I ended each letter the same way, always vaguely embarrassed that I was clinging to the pretense I should long since have abandoned: *P.S. No sign of you-know-who.*

When I told Grandpa that Luke would arrive within a week, he informed me that he was also taking a trip. He was going up to see Jacob, whose health had been deteriorating, and he could be away for a month this time. I didn't need to come; he would be visiting more frequently and I could accompany him another time. It only occurred to me much later to wonder if he'd deliberately left Luke and me alone.

On the day Luke was to arrive I woke up jittery, unsettled. He had bought a truck and was driving out, would be here before dark. I drank my morning tea and it made me even more restless. I packed a bag and set off up the mountain and into the next valley. The walk calmed me a bit; I enjoyed the contrast of climbing up the cool side of the mountain above our cabin and crossing over the ridge to the southwest aspect, into the well-spaced ponderosa pines with their sweet vanilla-scented bark, the flocks of jun-cos and chickadees flitting around importantly, and the sun, the gorgeous warm sun that soon became hot and oppressive. The huckleberries in the ava-lanche path were still hard and tinged greenish, but the saskatoons were perfect and I filled a cookie tin. I hiked back and had a long swim in our lake, ate stale bread and cold deer sausage for a late afternoon lunch on the porch. When the sun was low in the sky,

I walked back down to the lake and stood there, looking out at the water, feeling as though I was losing my mind with impatience. Then I heard Luke's truck; it sounded even worse than Grandpa's. I turned to walk up and meet him, but stopped. I wanted him to come and find me, and I wanted it to be right here, where we'd first met.

I heard his footsteps on the sand as he reached the beach, and I turned to see him. He was tanned and his dark hair was longer and bleached lighter by the sun. He wore a faded T-shirt and I remembered its softness under my fingers when I'd found it in his backpack. At the memory of that I looked away, and he walked over to me.

"This is for you," he said, reached around to pull something from his back pocket. A long, dark feather.

I pretended to scrutinize the feather. "Hmm… ivory-billed woodpecker?" I said, and he smiled.

"Heron," he said, as I reached to take it. "They live right in the city, along the ocean. It flew over me and I saw the feather as it was falling. I almost caught it before it touched down."

I stroked the edges of the feather delicately, to preserve its shape.

"Sure it's not one of your own?" I asked, then inwardly winced. I'd been aiming for an ironic tone but it came out tentatively. I wasn't sure he'd catch my clumsy reference and felt suddenly shy.

He caught my eye and a quick grin lit his face, then he shook his head, assumed an "above all that" countenance.

"I don't know what you're talking about," he said, looking away. "I really must apologize, though, for my current appearance. I don't normally go around like this, with nearly all my fur missing."

He held out his arm and turned it over, squinting at it critically, then patted at his head with both hands as though reassured to find his hair still there.

I shook my head but felt myself smiling, and he leaned down and slipped his bare foot out of his shoe, looked at it as though for the first time.

"I don't know how you humans manage to walk *anywhere* on these *tiny* little—"

He cut off as I playfully shoved his shoulder, which knocked him off balance. I was surprised by his strength and my own inadvertent shriek of laughter as he grabbed on to me and we both toppled to the sand. He made a show of helping me up, and then we just stood there, looking at each other. His expression was so open and earnest that I felt my breath catch. I closed my eyes for a moment, then looked at him again and still couldn't think of a thing to say, so instead I took a step forward and leaned into him and he wrapped his arms around me so swiftly and smoothly it was as though he'd been waiting. He smelled of cedar and musk and his neck was warm. I could feel his heart beating against my chest and I felt strangely calm. A dipper called out as it swooped past low over the water, and I heard the distant cries of the juvenile osprey that lurked in the trees around their nest, still haranguing their exhausted parents. The sun dropped below the mountains and the air was suddenly cooler. Overhead, the crows were flying home. I straightened up and took Luke's hand.

"Let's go," I said lightly, and we walked together up the path to the cabin.

WE TALKED LATE INTO THE night and then fell asleep together on the couch. I woke early, slipped from under Luke's arm, made myself a cup of tea and settled into the chair with my book, but I couldn't concentrate, kept glancing over at Luke. We hadn't so much as kissed, but something had shifted between us and I could begin to see the new trajectory we were setting out on, thrilling and inevitable at once.

He woke and we ate saskatoon-berry pancakes. We walked down to the lake and the fish were jumping, so we decided to take the canoe out. We crossed the length of the lake and tied on to the raft, which was anchored near the far end, then fished while the air and water slowly warmed up.

"I'm going for a swim," I said. I'd worn my bathing suit under my shorts and T-shirt, and I felt him watching as I peeled off my clothes and jumped in. I swam far out from the raft, and lingered there, treading water and watching him. The boat was tied up out of my line of vision and in its absence Luke looked somehow mysterious, a boy on a dock out in a lake, dry and clothed and far from shore. I swam back toward the raft, and when I was nearly there he mimed casting his hook out toward me, watching my struggle and leap high into the air, then his focused effort to reel me in. When I swam up to the dock, he set down his rod and reached out to help me climb up.

"You're a madman," I said, but accepted his hand. When I set my bare feet down on the sun-warmed wood of the dock and caught his eye, he was studying me so intently, so knowingly and affectionately, that I had to look down. I lifted my foot and set it lightly down on his tanned bare foot, took a deep breath and met his eyes. I steeled myself for just an instant before I leaned forward and kissed him.

He surprised me by not being tentative, by seeming, rather, as though he knew exactly what he was doing. After a moment I pulled back and regarded him appraisingly. Who knew what he'd gotten up to in the city, with the no doubt more sophisticated girls there? He pulled me back toward him and I hesitated, then decided not to think about his city life, for now. Nothing to do with me, with us. I closed my eyes and leaned into him, my friend, this stranger, Luke.

TWENTY-THREE

THE RIDGE HAS FLATTENED OUT, and I welcome the chance to tuck my poles under my arms and try to warm my hands. A few yards in front of me, a small weasel pokes its head out of the snow and stares at me in a manner I can only describe as insouciant. It scampers across the surface, revealing a luscious winter coat and a short, black-tipped tail, and plunges back into the snow a dozen yards from where it emerged. I am gratified by this glimpse of a predator, however diminutive. Something in their manner, so different from that of a prey species, always cheers me; that unperturbed cockiness. Once, when I was small, a juvenile northern saw-whet owl smashed into my loft window and stunned itself. The sound woke me up and Grandpa went and retrieved it, brought it up onto the porch to show me. I exclaimed over how cute the tiny, dazed owl was, and as it came back to its senses I was struck by its remarkable composure. I gingerly touched the bit of white on its forehead while it blinked at me calmly, fearlessly, until Grandpa told me to get on with it. Then I did what he'd instructed: I held on to its furry feet, lifted my hand high and released it into the night.

I come onto a more exposed stretch and the snow is so firm that my snowshoes barely penetrate. The wind-affected surface squeaks under each step, until I am once again surrounded by stunted subalpine firs, an occasional whitebark pine, and my steps sink deeply once more. I startle a flock of dull winter goldfinches from their roost and they rise up in a chirping, affronted mass and swoop off together, landing farther down the ridge.

There is a break in the line of tracks up ahead, and I rush forward. A gap of fifteen or twenty feet, but otherwise no change in the gait pattern. I stare at the space for a moment, then crouch down to look more closely at the surface of the snow and discover the faint marks of a tiny mouse or vole barely penetrating it.

I straighten up and skirt around the almost-bare stretch, reluctant to disturb it. I continue following Charlie's trail along the broad curving ridge. Visibility is worsening and I can't see across the valley to the mountains on the other side.

I stop, look up at the sky. The day is half gone. I have my headlamp, and the bright snow will help, but being out alone at night is a different prospect from what I've been doing so far. I've been following Charlie's roundabout trail but there's a much more direct route back to the cabin from here; if it comes to it, I can take a steeper line down the heavily forested slope on my left and, assuming I don't break an ankle on the shortcut, be home in no time.

There's a watch in my pack, if I really want to know the time, but it doesn't matter; the exact length of daylight remaining is of less concern than the heavy clouds moving in. Any significant snowfall will slow me down and increase the risk of being out here, and also reduce the chances of my catching up to Charlie. It will take a lot of snow to fill in his deep tracks, but I don't know how far ahead he is.

The ridge begins to climb again and I can't see beyond the next thirty yards of Charlie's trail. Suppose he's right there, beyond that rise? Sensing the change in air pressure, maybe, hunkering down in anticipation of a storm? I pull on a waterproof jacket, and open up the underarm zips so I don't overheat while I'm hiking, then grasp my poles and start up the ridge. My heart pounds faster until I see that there's nothing beyond the rise except snow, trees and more tracks leading farther along the ridge. The air is silent. Not only the usual muffled quiet of a snow-covered landscape; nothing is moving out here. No distant bird calls, no scratch of claws on bark. Everything is on hold, ready to wait it out—everything except one middle-aged female human. I tilt my head back and a snowflake lands on my face, then another. I lower my head and walk faster, the soft swish and thud of my snowshoes and poles unnaturally loud in the cooling air.

TWENTY-FOUR

LUKE'S FACE HID NOTHING FROM me. Every impulse, small joy or worry revealed itself, if only briefly; he was astonishingly without pretense. From being alone so much, I thought, from never being a child among children, never having to hide. But then I thought of his father and shook my head, gave up my analysis for the moment. He was inexplicable, and against all evidence to the contrary I believed myself the only young woman to ever have felt exactly as I did. I would wake in the night, thinking about him. I lost my appetite, caught myself staring into space, smiling. Of course, I told him none of this, not at first. I revealed my hand slowly, but in the end I held back nothing: a feat I've never had the inclination to repeat.

IT WAS THE END OF August now and the air had a new coolness to it, the laziness of summer sharpening into a growing sense of urgency. The osprey and kingfishers were fishing intently; the bears passing through from the wetlands to the neighbouring huckleberry-rich valley looked heftier every day; the squirrels tore seeds from cones in a frenzy of activity and shrieked indignantly at each other as they raced up and down the thick tree trunks. Luke and I lay side by side on our raft, still anchored near the back end of the lake— we were finally dried off from the long, cold swim to get there and in no hurry to jump back in.

I leaned up on my elbow and looked at him, appraisingly. I was well aware of the risks—knew that, inconveniently, girls my age tended to be outrageously fertile—but Luke and I had been alone at the cabin for a couple of weeks now, and my resolve was growing weak. Grandpa would return before long, and our as-yet-unconsummated teenage honeymoon would be over. This knowledge weighed heavily on me. There was one more thing I wanted to do, consequences be damned. I was a grown woman, or nearly enough.

"Do you—" I said, and stopped, tried again. "Are you sure you're not leaving anytime soon?"

"Absolutely not," he said. "In fact, I am planning to stay…" he raised himself up on one arm and squinted at his watch-less wrist, "at *least* another half-hour. Then I'll be out of your hair, for good."

I snorted and shook my head.

"Or we could get married," he said.

I gawked at him and he said, "Right now. Really, I mean it."

"Jesus Christ, Luke!" I said, shocked. Of course the thought of marriage had occurred to me, but I imagined that to be part of some distant future, not a topic to be broached here on the raft.

"I don't want to leave, Sandy," he said. "I've seen enough, out there. It's… it's not for me. This is where I want to be. Here, with you."

"We'll discuss that another time," I said firmly, and moved closer so I could feel his whole body stretched out against mine. When he turned toward me his chest was dry and sun-warmed, his back cooler from being against the damp wood of the dock. He pulled my hips toward him, I pressed against him and felt his swift response. My blood seemed to grow warmer, under that hot sun, and he kissed my neck in a way that brought me even more acutely into the present. A pair of entangled dragonflies alighted briefly on his shoulder before flying off across the lake, and Luke pulled back. He made a bit of a show of watching the dragonflies disappear, and when he turned to me his expression was so direct and lustful and pleading, all at once, that I swiftly decided to spare him the question and just answer it.

"Yes," I said.

Within a few moments he had manoeuvred me out of my bikini top, and even though we were the only people for miles around I felt too exposed out there. I pulled away and pointed to the almost-hidden glade beside the rockfall.

"Look," I said. "See that lonely patch of moss?"

"Achingly lonely," he said, pulling me back toward him. "Desperately. I can feel it from here."

It seems impossible, now, how young we were, how recently we had been children together. I stood on the dock for a moment, and watched him tread water as he waited for me. I jumped in and when I entered the cold water there was a sense of momentousness about it, anchoring my almost giddy anticipation as we swam to shore.

The moss was cool, damp and alive under us, twined through with fragrant twinflower and wild ginger. I shivered and Luke pulled me close to him while I pushed second thoughts from my mind. I kissed him, opened my eyes to find him watching me.

"Are you sure?" he said, and I nodded, slowly, struck speechless by my own daring.

I remember the warmth of our skin and the coolness of the air, my delight in his strong body and focused gaze. There was a moment of stinging pain when he finally pushed through into me and he hesitated when he saw the shock of it register on my face, and I gave a shake of my head to say *It's okay, don't stop*. The light was fading fast as dusk came on, the crows were calling overhead and I was completely absorbed in him: his weight on me, the soft moss beneath us, the scent of wild ginger on damp skin.

THE LATE SUMMER DAYS WERE long, and we made the most of them. I loved the fearless way Luke held my gaze, and the feel of the nape of his neck under my hand, his stubble against my face. And it gave me a thrill to be away from him—away, but in range. If I was out in the boat, idly watching the goldeneyes and mergansers, I couldn't resist occasionally turning the lenses of the binoculars toward Luke back on the shore, fishing or working on the raft, which he claimed to be building a raised bed frame onto so that we could spend nights out on the lake. Grandpa extended his trip to do some research at the university, allowing the two of us another few weeks alone. Most mornings I woke up first, and would watch Luke sleeping—the sense of distance was implied rather than literal but somehow satisfying in the same way. I was a very young woman, and I loved this very young man in all the usual ways that were, to me, astounding—a revelation. Grandpa called early one morning to say he would be back the following week, and hearing his voice in the cabin, while Luke slept up in my loft, made me a bit nervous about his return.

I climbed the ladder and sat on the bed, stroked Luke's hair to see if he'd wake up. He flung an arm around my waist, smiled sleepily and tried to pull me back into bed.

"Not a chance," I said. "Are you going to sleep all day?"

"Mm, brilliant idea," he said, and then I relented briefly and climbed into bed with him for a few minutes, but when he started to pull at my clothes I pushed him off.

"Grandpa's coming back next week," I said. "I think we should clean up your old cabin."

Since his return, we hadn't explicitly discussed what had happened in that cabin. I felt bad bringing it up but there was no way around it.

He saw me watching him, worriedly, and he smiled wryly. "My mom made me see a shrink every couple weeks for a year after that," he said. "I'm okay, Sandy."

I studied him a moment, unsure.

"Let's do it," he said. "We can start this morning. How bad can it be? A few mice, maybe a pack rat, or ten?"

"Or maybe Charlie's moved in and is studying the bizarre habits of his human neighbours," I suggested.

"If only," he said. I narrowed my eyes and studied him for a moment, and concluded that he was dead serious.

WE PUSHED OPEN THE DOOR to his old cabin, and the air was stale but not as much as I'd expected. Luke stared at the floor, and I saw where Grandpa had replaced the bloodstained floorboards. The cabin was nearly empty; Grandpa had originally built it with the idea that my mother could have it when she was grown, and it hadn't even been furnished until Luke and Eva arrived. They'd come here with almost nothing, and before they left they'd packed everything up, either to take with them or to give away. The two twin beds were there, each in its own small bedroom, and a few pots and pans, but not much else.

We took the boards off the windows, and the light flooding in showed how much dust we had to deal with. We caught three mice and a pack rat the first night the traps were out—dead, the pack rat was dismayingly adorable, but at least it seemed to be the only one. We scrubbed the place down, marvelling at the extravagance of cobwebs, the tiny sprouts growing in the thin strip of grime behind the kitchen sink. We took the mattresses off the beds and pushed them together on the floor in the main room. Luke cleaned out the wood stove and chimney, and I sewed new curtains for the few small windows. We didn't quite have the gall to move all my things over from the other cabin, but we began to spend every night there.

Grandpa came back, but said he'd be heading up north again soon; Jacob was not recovering as hoped. Grandpa took in the new affection between Luke and me without a word, but looked pleased as he clasped Luke's hand, and startled me by telling me I had grown up just beautifully. On his second night back, he woke up as I was sneaking out to go to Luke's, and said into the darkness, "Sandy, please. Spare me the subterfuge, it's really not necessary."

I stood, frozen, unsure how to respond. "Well. Alrighty then," I said, my face burning. "I'll, uh, see you in the morning."

He didn't reply and I slipped out the door, wondering if he could possibly have fallen back asleep so quickly. The moon lit the clearing and I didn't need my flashlight as I ran lightly up the path.

I APPLIED TO RUN THE swimming instruction program at the new indoor pool in town, and Luke found work on a building site for a new supermarket, just a few blocks away from the pool. We drove to town together every workday, an hour-long trip with the radio crackling into the truck for the last stretch, once we could pick up a signal. I finished work first so I would walk over to his worksite at the end of the day. I liked to walk over stealthily, see how close I could get before he caught me sneaking up on him. If the day was at all warm, his shirt would be off, his jeans resting below his hipbones, pulled down by the weight of tools slung through his belt. Drawing near, I watched his arms straining as he carried stacks of two-by-sixes, his careful squint as he measured and sawed. The sweet, smoky smell of sawdust lingered on his skin and clothes through the long drive home each afternoon. We sometimes went for a walk before one of us or Grandpa made dinner. Luke would often stay at our cabin for the evening and then retire to his own. Sometimes I went over there with him, but I was used to solitude and sometimes liked having a bed to myself, so I didn't abandon my loft entirely. One night Luke headed back to his place and I sat reading on the couch, and Grandpa came out of his office and said there was something he'd been meaning to talk to me about.

"An old colleague called a few days ago to let me know there's a temporary teaching position available in the biology department, starting in January," he said.

He looked a bit nervous, but mostly excited as he continued. "They don't have a veterinary program, of course, I'd just be teaching a few zoology courses. I got in touch and the position is mine, if I want it. I always liked the town—you know I worked up there on and off for years—and it would give me more time to spend with Jacob. I hadn't thought to leave you alone here, but now—" He didn't finish, he didn't need to. A seventeen-year-old girl alone for the winter was one thing, but with two of us it was entirely possible. I was comfortable enough with the propane appliances that Grandpa didn't even have to get involved anymore when the old stove acted up. Luke already knew how to manage the water system, and, more importantly, he had the patience and skill to engineer creative solutions to the many issues that could arise with the various pieces of hardware that kept us going.

"Well," I said slowly, "that would be a big change."

He waited for me to go on, and I felt a rush of affection for him. I hadn't given enough thought to how he'd put his whole life on hold for me; I supposed children never did. It had been ten years since he'd worked regularly, and he was only seventy, still mentally and physically strong.

"I suppose I've monopolized your not-inconsiderable teaching ability for long enough," I sighed. I walked over and embraced him, for a moment, where he sat in his chair. His hair was thin on top, and at some point in the last few years it had completely changed to silver without my noticing. He was a handsome old bastard, still. Maybe he had a secret girlfriend up north.

ONE DAY AT THE END of October, we came home to hear Grandpa on the radio phone. He was talking to a woman who sounded middle-aged, and I elbowed Luke meaningfully, having shared my idle daydream about Grandpa finding love again. The tone of their goodbyes didn't fit my speculation, though, and when he switched the phone off and turned to us he had an air of anxiety. He told us it was Jacob's eldest daughter; she'd called because Jacob wasn't doing well. She didn't think this was the end, but she thought Grandpa would want to know, in case he wanted to come early. I felt a pang of incipient grief, and told myself that Jacob was strong and would be okay. Grandpa was clearly thrown off by the news, and uncharacteristically fretful.

"We've got enough wood," he said, "but I'd hoped to get more propane next week. One of you will have to go—for the love of God, be *sure* the tanks are well secured. And I haven't shown Luke how to manage the plow yet, Sandy; the two of you will have to sort it out. It could snow anytime now, but I didn't think—" he cut off, his face stricken. "I just thought there was more time."

Grandpa left on a chilly morning in early November, the sound of his truck growing more distant until I only imagined I could still hear it. Luke and I went out walking that afternoon; our breath made clouds in the frigid air, and crystalline fingers of hoarfrost protruded like icy flowers from the frozen ground, crunching under our boots. We walked out onto the lake, silently admiring the stark beauty around us.

"Oh!" Luke said, suddenly. "I just had the strangest feeling that I've been here before—that we stood right here, and everything was exactly the same."

"Déjà vu," I said, and when he looked at me inquiringly, I gave him a look—was he really unfamiliar with the term? "You know, it's French," I clarified. "It means 'already seen.'"

He stared thoughtfully out across the frozen lake. "There's a word for it? And all this time, I thought it only happened to me."

I looked at him, wondering, but before I could give it much thought, he continued.

"What about when you are sleeping, having a dream, but you know you're dreaming? Is there a word for that?"

"Lucid dreaming, I think," I said.

"I think I do both at once," he said. "I'll know I'm dreaming, and I have the feeling of déjà vu at the same time." He pronounced the French term without any trouble—I should have known he was messing with me.

"One of the girls from the pool thinks you can meet up with people in your dreams," I said, and he raised an eyebrow.

"Well, if that's the case then I hope you don't get tired of me," he shrugged, "because I intend to spend every waking *and* dreaming moment with you."

I rolled my eyes, but stepped into his arms. I would never say the things he did, and I marvelled, not for the first time, that we were even the same species. It was a cold night, but we were alone and seventeen, and Luke, boy scout that he was, had packed a thick blanket, which he now laid out hopefully on the snow.

WITH GRANDPA AWAY, WE BOTH stayed in the larger cabin, as it had more space and the better cookstove. I liked bustling around in the morning, making breakfast with Luke sleeping upstairs in my loft. By December, we were driving home from work in the dark to a cabin that had grown cold in our absence. We stoked up the fire and snuggled under blankets on the couch, hot mugs of tea warming our fingers while the cabin heated back up.

Some nights we walked out into the dark and lay on our backs on the frozen lake, watching the northern lights flickering and dancing on their cedar-fringed stage until we got too cold and ran back to the cabin, panting and laughing as we raced up the path. We talked about Neil Armstrong walking on the moon the previous summer, about the rumour that Neil Young was going to play a show on the coast that spring. One night I told him how I'd seen a woman in town that morning, from a distance: a tall woman with long red hair and a familiar gait. My heart had surged and I believed, for a flickering moment, that I was seeing my mother, just ahead of me on the street, and without thinking I began to run to catch up with her. Before I reached her, the woman turned to go into a store and I saw her face, her stranger's face, and I stopped on the street, numb with disappointment, while people kept moving around me.

Another night, Luke told me that something Grandpa had said about Charlie was stuck in his head, and he couldn't shake it. Grandpa had told Luke that, as he grew older, he became increasingly convinced that Charlie was something other than an ordinary animal. "The behaviours, even the appearances, seem to vary wildly. Either there are several distinct species of bipedal primates between the coast and the Rockies, or the creatures appear differently to different people," Grandpa had said. "Surely the former is less unlikely than the latter, but I just keep circling back to the idea that they are, somehow, both real *and*—" Luke told me that Grandpa stopped there, and seemed to search for a word, but then said he was still trying to work it out.

I gave it some thought. It was true that I couldn't explain the uncanny feeling I had experienced when I had stood before Charlie's tracks that winter day when I was twelve, nor could any of us make sense of the vanishing of his trail, as reported by both Grandpa and Luke, but I felt both of them took it all too far. They seemed to bring out, in each other, an inclination toward the irrational, though I had always understood Grandpa's tendency to be symbolic, a post-religious tic. As for Luke, well, that was another thing entirely.

"Don't you think that, really, it's most likely that Charlie is just an enterprising ape who decided to stroll across the Bering Strait?" I asked. "Just a very rare flesh-and-blood animal?" Then, affectionately performing my best Grandpa, I added, "It is vital to hold firm to the distinction between one's hopes and one's perceptions, *especially* when the line between them is so fine as to be almost imperceptible."

I was pretty sure I'd said that wrong, but Luke didn't seem to notice.

"No," Luke said, and pulled me toward him, "*you* are so fine as to be almost imperceptible."

"What you just said is absolute nonsense, on so many levels," I said. I didn't know how I could possibly have fallen in love with this man, but there was no arguing with the fact that I had.

GRANDPA RETURNED IN THE MIDDLE of February in 1970, just in time for my eighteenth birthday. He stayed only for the weekend, and Luke and I were alone when he turned eighteen, a week after I did. Grandpa called at the end of March to tell us Jacob had died, surrounded by his family. Despite having known he was critically ill, I was shocked at the news. We'd visited over Christmas and he'd seemed much the same as always. Even when he moved into the hospital in February, I still clung to a firm belief that he would recover. Having never been witness to slow death from illness, I had imagined Jacob lounging comfortably on a hospital bed, looking just as he had so many times on our sofa, gesticulating elegantly as he described whatever legal challenge was currently absorbing his attention.

Luke and I took the train up north for the funeral. I looked out the window as the scenery streamed past and imagined Jacob as a tiny baby, riding a train in the arms of a stranger, being carried away from his family, his history. When I was small I imagined that our shared lack of parents made us alike, and only later did I even begin to understand that our challenges were entirely different in scope and scale. What else had I failed to notice, to understand of his life, the complex struggles and varied joys of his particular existence? The train continued on, the sunlight briefly flickering off and on as we sped through a narrow, high-walled passage, carved by dynamite through walls of stone.

GRANDPA CAME BACK IN THE spring for a visit, and told us he had news.

"A permanent teaching position has come up at the university," he said, and caught my gaze. "I've accepted it. I found a small house for rent, just a short walk from campus. It all feels very opportune."

I didn't know how to feel. Of course, I wanted to be here with Luke, but I didn't want Grandpa to move away entirely, either.

"I thought I was long done with academic life," he said, "but perhaps it's not yet done with me. And besides, I'm getting too old for this place. You two are managing just fine without me."

Now that he was moving away on a more long-term basis, Grandpa wanted to show us where he kept all the important papers, "just in case." I hadn't thought much about that side of things, and felt like he was giving us an abrupt crash course in adulthood. There was the insurance for the cabin, though God willing we were not foolish enough to forget to clean the chimney and cause the place to burn down in his absence. Here was the phone number of a fellow named Elijah, who could come in and fix the gas stove *only* if it was well and truly broken and not just being curmudgeonly. He told us where and how to pay the property taxes, and made sure we had the contact information for annual contributions to the scholarship foundation Jacob had set up a few years earlier, for Indigenous students who wanted to attend law school but faced financial barriers.

Despite these preparations, Grandpa's departure felt abrupt, and I alternately missed him and felt a new, adult freedom with his absence. Luke and I had made friends in town, and sometimes other young couples would come out and visit us at the cabin, bringing guitars and wine and occasionally marijuana. We planted a few hardy vegetables, chopped the firewood we'd felled and bucked the previous year, and later harvested the garden, along with the apples and wild berries, canning and drying what we could for winter. Winter arrived, Grandpa came back for Christmas and then left again. We turned nineteen, winter melted into spring, and we were married twice—once down at the lake, with Grandpa officiating and a few of our new friends present, and then officially, at the registrar's office in town. In the style of the time, I took Luke's surname: I was now Cassandra Linnea Russo.

When the weather warmed, we spent most weekends out exploring the area in Luke's old truck, finding remote lakes to camp at, barely getting a moment's sleep in his old tent. On the edge of a marshy lake at a highway rest stop we followed an oddly sweet chirpy call and found a party of toads, paired off and spawning so listlessly that they could have been dead but for the occasional calls that seemed to be issuing from the males, and the strings of eggs emerging slowly from the larger, bloated females. On a hike up the sunny western aspect of a nearby mountain, we saw a pair of alligator lizards, one's jaws clamped around the other's neck as they scurried along in what may have been mating behaviour, or attempted cannibalism. As we lay chatting in the sun at the top, a mountain chickadee plucked a piece of fluff from the sweater I'd just removed and flew off to show its mate. Everywhere we went, robins hopped along trails in front of us, industriously gathering tiny twigs to shore up their nests.

On a cold, moonlit night in February of 1973, I dreamed that I stood at a mirror and watched, aghast, as all of my teeth crumbled in my jaws. I woke with a start, and sat up in bed with an unpleasant, chalky taste in my mouth. I felt both starved and nauseous, and I shivered and pulled the blankets around me, my heart suddenly speeding up. I didn't consider for a moment that I might be coming down with something; my period was two weeks late, my breasts swollen and sore. I hadn't told Luke, waiting for a clearer sign, but at that moment I knew. The back of my throat tightened and I swallowed, hard.

Moonlight shone through the window onto Luke's face as he slept. It had always been just the two of us, alone together. I had wanted this to happen, but felt suddenly and acutely apprehensive about what it would mean for us. When we were small, we would play happily together all day, every day, for whole weeks, months—whole *years*, it seemed. We had no one else, and we needed no one else. Each day when the sun slipped behind the mountains, and the air was suddenly cooler and the crows began to fly home, there would be Grandpa's distinctive whistle or the ringing of Eva's dinner bell and we would wake from our shared dream of pirates or soldiers and run toward our respective homes without so much as a word of farewell—never slowing down, never looking back. I lightly traced the lines of my husband's face, wondered what features we would each give our child, and what it would take from us in return.

TWENTY-FIVE

THE SNOW HAS STARTED IN earnest. There is no wind and the large flakes fall straight down, perfect stellars landing on my sleeves. The snow that has already fallen would neatly erase a vole's tracks, and if it continues at this rate it would cover a snowshoe hare's within the hour. I imagine myself standing alone among the trees with Charlie's trail covered over completely, my own tracks slowly filling in behind me. The image brings me back to the dream that woke me this morning.

I dreamed of my mother often after I lost her, but I can't seem to capture Luke the same way. He eludes me, flits around the edges of my dreams, slips in only to immediately become someone else so that I hardly have a chance to really take in his presence. There is only one dream, a recurring one, in which he is really present, fully himself. It is a winter night. The sky is clear, and hoarfrost crystals sparkle in the moonlight. We stand together on a small rise of land in an open conifer forest. We hold each other's mittened hands, and I lean into him but can't feel his warmth through our heavy wool coats. After a few minutes I realize there are no tracks in the snow around us, no indication of how we got there, or from what direction. I turn to point this out to Luke but he just smiles con-spiratorially, and raises a finger to his lips. I stare at him, and comprehension swoops down but before it can land I am suddenly awake.

I've dreamed this scene half a dozen times, maybe more. I dreamed it when I was twenty-five with both kids snuggled in bed with me, and when I was close to forty, on a stolen night in the home of a new lover. And, after a long time of not dreaming of Luke, or my mother, but of houses—crumbling old mansions with bookshelves built over secret passageways, flimsy treehouses built at exhilarating heights in ancient cedars—I dreamed it again, last night. Luke raised his finger to his lips, and then I was woken by the hapless sparrow downstairs, thudding into the window as it tried to escape through solid glass. And outside, the enormous footprints were laid out across the clearing, clear as day in the fresh snow.

TWENTY-SIX

FINALLY, ONE OF THE SPAWNING kokanee salmon managed to clear the small set of rapids, and Luke turned to me with a look of delight. I, too, felt a momentary surge of vicarious triumph for the hardworking fish and, not to be left out, our unborn child punched my bladder and ground its heel against my ribs. I was seven months along and the baby's movements had changed in tenor—no more backflips, just intermittent, forceful kicks and shoves, heralding an imminent desire for escape.

We were at a provincial park a few hours from home; it was warmer than our cool, narrow valley where the summer heat had largely exited the scene, appearing only in teasing flashes for a few glorious and somehow bittersweet moments at a time. I was enjoying the mid-September sun on my bare arms, the sounds of the fast-moving creek and the songbirds flitting through the deciduous bushes over our heads, calling out to each other in their melodious, oversized voices.

The kokanee rested in pools between forward surges, transformed by spawning from sleek, silvery little numbers to a startling shade of red, their heads a pleasing olive green. The dead among them, presumably having completed their mission, littered the shore, picked apart by industrious crows. Mallards drifted to and fro in unhurried circles, tipping themselves bottom-up to snack on the eggs the salmon had just deposited in the pebbles lining the creek bed. Fifty yards upstream, a black bear ambled through the shallow water, feeding indiscriminately on the dead and the dying. Despite the natural beauty, there was something of the battlefield about the entire scene.

I asked Luke if he remembered the time Grandpa brought us here as children, when Luke had tried to chase the mallards off from eating the salmon eggs, while I argued strenuously in favour of the ducks and tried to physically restrain him. Luke countered that I had once convinced him to sneak an egg from Johannsen's coop and carry it around inside his shirt day and night, with predictable results.

"I most certainly did *not* tell you to do that," I said. "Does that sound like me? I'm sure that was *all* you."

He paused, thinking. "Maybe you're right," he said, and with a logic apparent only to himself he continued, "I must be mixing it up with that other time, when you gave me the bad news about Santa."

Even as I opened my mouth, formulating a denial, a shadowy memory surfaced. We were seven, standing in the clearing in front of his cabin on a snowy afternoon. Luke excitedly described the new toboggan Santa was going to bring him on Christmas morning and I glanced at him sharply, smugly incensed that he was still a believer. I couldn't remember the exact words I employed to relieve him of his illusion, but I remembered his face when I said it. "You're lying," he said, his voice shrill with sudden doubt, his eyes wounded. "You're a liar!" Snow swirling around us, an incomplete snowman standing witness.

I looked at him now, remembered the weighty sense of defensive righteousness I had felt, and shrugged.

"Wasn't me," I said. "Must have been one of those little assholes next door."

Luke smiled at the reference to my imaginary childhood scapegoats.

"You were so *ferocious* back then," he said, his tone more wistful than accusing.

Luke had been idly flipping over rocks, and he swiftly scooped something up. He turned to me, hands cupped around it, and his face bore an expression I'd seen so many times before that I smiled, even before I saw what this particular treasure was.

It looked like a slightly oversized earthworm—or, rather, like the fake worms, designed for use as bait, that I'd once seen in a fishing shop. I stared a moment, baffled, then it slithered forward and raised the front half of its body gracefully up from his hand.

"A rubber boa," he said. "I've only seen them in books."

I hadn't seen one either—we didn't have any around our place, as far as I knew—but I remembered that it was a constrictor and not venomous. He tipped it into my hand and it rested on the warmth of my palm with that vaguely solipsistic disinclination to escape I'd often noted in small reptiles and amphibians, once they were in hand. The snake's mouth opened, its tongue flicked rapidly in and out. I tilted my hand slightly and it coiled around my index finger and squeezed—more strongly than I'd anticipated, hinting at an incipient threat. Faintly disturbed, I set the snake down and watched it disappear into the rocks.

A splash from the creek caught our attention as a particularly beat-up kokanee leapt up and crashed against the rocks. The current pushed it backwards; it spun around and stalled in a back eddy. After a moment's pause, it reoriented itself facing upstream and began to inch slowly forward against the current— as though, sheer exertion having failed, it was now attempting to conquer the rapids by stealth.

"There's just something so compelling about their life cycle," Luke said. "The circularity of it; how they spawn and then immediately die. It's kind of perfect, in a way."

I looked at him, my hand resting on my pregnant belly, and shook my head incredulously. Really, the man had no sense of timing whatsoever.

WE DROVE HOME ALONG THE narrow highway, Luke behind the wheel where I could no longer fit with much comfort. Trying to redeem his salmon envy, he told me that he kept experiencing moments of inexplicable certainty that our baby possessed some kind of "magic powers." I coolly suggested he might wish to temper his expectations. He reached over to stroke my hair, told me I looked beautiful in my breeding plumage. I told him that made no sense at all, but I didn't resist when he started to rub my neck.

We weren't long into our drive when I remembered the parcel from Eva in the backseat. I retrieved it with some difficulty and tore into it. On top was an envelope containing a pair of crayoned drawings made by Luke and I as young children. I had drawn a picture of myself in the "early childhood realistic" style: I was up in the observatory tower, my hand raised in a wave, with a squirrel—also waving—perched on my shoulder. In Luke's self-portrait, he was fishing off the shoreline. He'd done a good, careful job on the tree-covered mountains in the background, but what caught the eye was his long, emerald-green tail. Until now, I'd forgotten all about his imaginary tail; for an entire fall and winter, he had insisted it was a real appendage that he actually—albeit invisibly—possessed. He drove us all nuts, insisting that room be made for it on the sofa, shrieking if anybody "stepped on it," until somebody finally grabbed the tail and cut it off with a pair of scissors. One of those little assholes next door, no doubt.

I dug through crumpled newspaper, found a tiny, hand-knitted cardigan and yet another pregnancy manual. *Getting a bit late for that now*, I thought, but flipped through it anyway.

"Look at this!" I snorted. "There's a sidebar on the dangers of eating raw eggs during pregnancy, and they called it 'Et Tu, Caesar Salad?' I can't believe she keeps sending these things."

"I can't believe you keep reading them," he said.

"You know, *salmonella* is actually kind of a pretty word," I said. "I would almost add it to the list of girls' names, if I didn't know what it meant."

"How about *pneumonia*?" he suggested. "Only spell it N-a-m-o—"

He cut off as a squirrel darted out onto the road in front of us, and he swerved to avoid it. We rounded a bend and there was a crow in our lane; it flew up reluctantly, at the last moment, from the body of another, less-lucky squirrel. It was a very fresh and messy kill and we were both silent as we reached the summit of the mountain pass and began the long, scenic descent. Late afternoon sun set the broad valley alight, drawing my gaze away from the sheer rocks that pressed tightly against the road on my side of the car. Millions of larch needles glowed golden-yellow; the effect was almost too dazzling. It was as though we were crossing a moat of liquid gold on a bridge that was winding and narrow, and possibly treacherous.

LUKE CALLED OUT FROM THE kitchen to ask if I needed a snack, and I didn't answer. On the sofa, on my throne of pillows, I seethed. He had told me he would make dinner, but he'd barely started and I was already starving and I would have *strongly* preferred to just do it myself, in a timely manner. He called out that he was bringing me some toast, but I was not placated. It seemed there was, within the murky depths of my psyche, an easily offended diva figure who had been awakened from dormancy by this pregnancy and now rose up periodically to assert her rather challenging presence. Mostly, I was able to keep my irrational reactions to myself. At this moment, though, I just felt too weary and put-upon by the unfairness of it.

"The unfairness of what?" Luke asked, when I tried to explain.

"Oh, just the unequal burden of reproduction between the sexes," I said, waving a hand dismissively. "Nothing for you to trouble your pretty little head over." I took a bite of the toast and it was good, and it wasn't easy making good toast over a gas burner, but I was still not happy.

"Sandy," he said, and his tone was sympathetic, but somehow infuriatingly so.

"I think I'll head to town for a bit," I announced, standing up.

Luke stood and reached for me but I stepped away, pulled on a sweater and walked outside. I wandered listlessly around the garden as a means of stalling. I imagined driving to town, alone, not because I really wanted to but because I'd stupidly said I would. It was almost dusk, not the best time to be on the road. Maybe, no—*probably*, something would run out in front of the car and I would swerve wildly but hit it anyway. Something massive and final: a moose or an elk or, even better, *Charlie*. I could bring about the end of his line and my own, in one fell swoop.

I picked a few shrivelled, raisiny saskatoons from the bushes at the garden's edge. What I suddenly wanted was to be sitting on a deck chair, sipping tea with my mother. I felt the sudden, hot invasion of tears and angled my head so that Luke wouldn't see, if he happened to be watching.

MID-MORNING THE FOLLOWING DAY I heard the car of my friend and midwife, Rachel, coming up the laneway, right on time. Luke was at work, and she'd told me she was coming by to visit, and also for my checkup.

"Christ," she said, when I met her at the edge of the clearing. "I can't believe you used to do that drive every day."

"Let's just stick with meeting in town from now on," I said. "Better foraging opportunities down there."

"Oh! Speaking of which," she said, and handed me a paper bag that smelled heavenly. I opened it to see two gorgeous chocolate croissants from the fancy new bakery in town.

"God bless you," I said, almost meaning it, and she acknowledged my invocation with an exaggerated queenly nod. The affectation rather suited her, I thought: Rachel was a curvy, dark-haired beauty from a large Italian-Doukhobor clan, and she was extremely comfortable giving orders, no doubt from years of ordering her brothers around. I felt sure she'd have no problem managing not only me, but also Luke and Grandpa, during the birth.

"Tea?" I offered. I stood up, and she waved me back into my seat.

"I'll get it," she said. "It's good to see you resting, for once." She looked at me again, more sharply.

"You just sat down when you heard my car, didn't you?" She glanced around the vicinity. "Aha!" She pointed to the basket that was half-full of the potatoes I'd been digging three minutes ago.

I shrugged, conceding the point. "I can't just sit around in a rocker, knitting woollen booties all day," I said.

"I doubt you've knitted a thing in your life," Rachel said, canny as always.

"I feel fine. I could still be at work every day," I said. "Did I tell you what they said, at the pool? 'We can't have you getting kicked in the stomach.' *Stomach*! As though the baby was, you know, my last *meal*."

Rachel had heard all this before, and calmly rummaged through her midwifery bag. She handed me a small strip of something like litmus paper. "You know what to do," she said, and I dutifully headed down the porch steps. I bypassed the outhouse because it was awkward to manoeuvre around in there, and squatted near the garden, admiring the leaves of the aspen and Douglas maples around me. Their colours grew more vibrant by the day as the leaves slowly painted themselves for courage, preparing to leap to their deaths.

I handed the urine test strip to Rachel and she looked at it approvingly. We went inside and she listened to the baby's heartbeat, then handed me the stethoscope so I could hear. We'd done this plenty of times by now but, as always, my breath caught at the sound of that rapid, steady patter. For me, this was when the baby's fragility was most alarmingly apparent: if a heart beats, it logically follows that it can *stop* beating. It was little comfort that I shared this trepidation with countless other pregnant women, past and present. Perhaps every first-time mother experiences something akin to what Galileo must have felt, upon concluding that everything he had once believed about the universe was wrong. The centre had shifted, the order of things was upended. Now, everything revolved around the fluttering of this tiny heart.

"Coming along beautifully," Rachel said, putting away her measuring tape. Then she looked at me. "What is it?"

"Everything will be okay, right?" I could hear the waver in my voice.

Her answering smile was one thread short of being reassuring: wry, sympathetic and fatalistic, all at once. I waited for the impossible guarantee that I knew she couldn't deliver.

"It is most likely that everything will be just fine," she said carefully, firmly.

I showed Rachel the crib that Eva had ordered for us to pick up at the new Sears outlet in town. I hadn't liked the stark, sterile look of the thing until I thought to paint it a beautiful, robin's egg blue. It was set up in the larger downstairs bedroom, the one I still thought of as Grandpa's. He'd moved his things into the smaller cabin when we told him I was pregnant, saying it was plenty of space for his occasional visits. "You can keep this fellow here, though," he'd said, patting Charlie's arm affectionately. "He'd be forever bumping his head over there."

Looking around the otherwise-empty bedroom, Rachel asked, "Are you still sleeping up in the loft?"

"That ladder," I said, "is *perfectly* safe." But I knew that, any day now, I would let Luke move us down from my beloved childhood loft, in what I imagined to be the final step in my acquiescence to the reality of motherhood. The tiny revolutionary inside me would overthrow my entire system. It would be a coup, and not a bloodless one.

AFTER RACHEL WENT BACK TO town I luxuriated in the still-novel experience of an effortless hot bath— the previous spring, Luke had provided us with the blessed miracle of on-demand water heaters for the kitchen and bathroom. After my bath I fell asleep on the sofa and woke, disoriented, in late afternoon when Luke opened the front door. The sense of being half-in and half-out of a dream stayed with me as he heated up leftover soup and served it to me on the sofa. The last light of day slipped away as I sipped honeyed nettle tea, my feet tucked under Luke as he played guitar. The softly lit cabin, the earthy sweetness of my tea and the sound of Luke's guitar and voice suddenly coalesced in a sense of déjà vu, which for me always bore a heavy but somehow comforting weight—not regret, exactly, but an acute awareness of the passage of time that carried within it an inherent sense of loss.

I closed my eyes and listened, feeling prematurely nostalgic as I imagined our future children lying in their beds, listening to Luke singing and playing as they succumbed to the deep sleep of childhood. But now, again, here it was, that creeping sense of menace stealing in to shadow my vision. Soon the baby would be out, and anything could happen. I would be endlessly vigilant, and my vigilance would guarantee nothing. Snakes lurked between sun-warmed rocks. Crows observed our desperate striving upstream with casual self-interest, and endless patience. All the while, the sun reflected prettily off the surface of the cold, swirling water, and birdsong filled the air. All of it so lovely, so fraught with blatant and hidden peril.

The baby was awake now, and rattling the bars of its cage, awaiting the day it would emerge and stake its claim. I pressed my hand against my belly to feel the outline of its knee, or foot. Its beautiful, emerald-green tail.

TWENTY-SEVEN

THE SNOWFALL SHOWS NO SIGN of letting up but then it generally doesn't, until it suddenly stops.

The sky is overcast, and the trees grow thicker along this part of the ridge, making it darker still. The snow in Charlie's tracks indicates that he's well ahead of me—unless he's been waiting, just ahead.

I pause: there's a scent in the air, strong and musky—as though a herd of elk is near—but heavier, with a hint of decay like the taste of a rotting tooth. I think, suddenly, of the black bear I came upon once, while I was hiking alone. I'd ascended onto a plateau and then froze when I saw it, just fifteen yards away, tearing into the stinking carcass of a deer. I carefully retreated, acutely aware of my physical vulnerability, my unnervingly close proximity to the sheer wild bulk of it.

The wooden Charlie sculpture has huge, strong hands and a powerful-looking jaw. How quickly could the real thing tear a person apart, with the slightest inclination? I inhale again and there is only the clean freshness of snow on conifers, but the feeling of foreboding stays with me as I follow Charlie's trail, as snow accumulates in his tracks and my own.

TWENTY-EIGHT

THE WINTER OF 1974 STARTED out with a mid-November cold snap, and we woke on the morning of Sam's first birthday to find the lake turned to glass. It was rare for it to freeze thickly before any significant snow fell, and Luke and I were gleeful as children, digging out our old skates. We skated all morning and then again after dinner and into the night; the cold air on our faces, the faintest trace of northern lights overhead, Sam babbling in delight from his cozy post in the baby backpack that Luke was wearing. I was a decent skater but too afraid of falling on Sam, my natural boldness somewhat tempered of late. The night was so clear that we felt certain we were seeing stars we'd never seen before and we pointed up at them, proposing names ranging from the pretty to the ridiculous. When we finally walked back to the cabin—holding each other's mittened hands, Sam asleep on Luke's back—I felt a pang of sympathy for the many humans who never get to experience the keen exhilaration of living amid snow and ice.

That was the start of our last winter together. I wish I could say that the memory provided some comfort to me later, but it came to feel like a vague, oblique warning that slipped past me, unnoticed. The squirrel was another such "sign," as I came to see it, a strange and sad little incident that later felt heavy with portent. It showed up a few months later, at the end of February, a time I thought of as near the end of winter though, at this elevation, it was nothing of the sort. I'd woken up naturally, opening my eyes to the sight of a sleeping baby rather than a hungry one: a rare and blessed occurrence. We had a sweet, easy morning; I bundled Sam up and let him toddle around the clearing, startling the chickadees with his shrill giggles, and while he napped after lunch I finally finished reading a novel that was already a week overdue at the town library. As I mashed carrots for Sam's afternoon snack I was tired, as usual, but not at all displeased with my lot.

Somehow, I didn't hear a sound from the squirrel, or see any sign that it had taken up residence, until I encountered the fluffy-tailed rodent itself. I opened a cupboard to get a clean bib for Sam and there it was, curled up in a pile of shredded tea towels. After a startled instant in which neither of us moved, the squirrel sprang up over my shoulder, crashed ungracefully onto the cabin floor and nearly flew across the room to hurl itself into the kindling box. Sam, in his high chair, let out a shrill squeal, pointing at the squirrel's hiding place with the delirious glee of a fifteen-month-old who finally has something significant to point at. I was considering how to get the squirrel out when I heard Luke on the porch, banging off his boots. I hoped it would make its escape when he opened the door, but no such luck.

Luke was sympathetic to what he assumed were the squirrel's honest efforts to prepare a nesting place.

"It's only February," I protested. "Surely it's not their breeding season?"

"They're rodents," he said. "They don't have a breeding season; any time will do."

At that, he produced an exaggerated seductive smile, to which I rolled my eyes and conceded that, in any case, the floor under Sam's high chair was so consistently and generously scattered with food scraps that the squirrel may well have decided to procreate out of season to take advantage of the rare bounty. I started to pull the kindling out of the box, but it soon became clear that the squirrel had escaped.

"Rat trap," I said offhandedly, just to get a reaction; Sam was ferociously mobile and we couldn't even keep mousetraps in their usual places. Luke had been encouraging Sam to eat his mashed carrots and he stopped, affected an appalled expression and sanctimoniously covered Sam's ears. Sam laughed, reaching his hand into the bowl.

"Well, set a live trap, then," I said. "I don't want everything getting chewed up."

The squirrel streaked across the floor, and Sam lost his mind with excitement. Orange mush everywhere.

"Come on, might be fun to keep it for a while," Luke said. I glanced sharply at him to see if he was serious and couldn't decide one way or the other.

"If I see it again, it'll be the slingshot," I said.

He insisted that he would find it and remove it safely, and I let him go about getting the flashlight, and a pillowcase, and a pair of leather gloves.

"You, my love, are an absolute nut," I said. "Saving up squirrels for the winter." I could hardly believe it when he managed to corner it under our bed, and seized it in his gloved hands.

Luke stood up, the struggling squirrel clasped in both hands, and Sam and I both stared, rapt, as it managed to squeeze halfway out of his grip. Then, it stopped moving. Its eyes bulged briefly and it fell limp. Startled, I looked at Luke to catch his eye but he was staring, aghast, at the squirrel. He slowly turned it over to reveal its blank glassy eyes. He held it in one hand and tore the glove off his other, laid his bare fingers on its torso. The look on his face confirmed it.

"Capture myopathy," I said, unnerved. I'd heard of it but never, before now, witnessed the phenomenon. Had a human appeared to succumb instantaneously at the very moment of capture it would have seemed a laughably transparent diversion tactic. But there was no question here: the squirrel was dead.

Luke continued to stare at it. "I didn't squeeze it tightly," he said, and paused. "I wonder if—" he began again, then stopped.

I could see that he was about to get into a reflective state over the unnecessary death, and I lacked the patience, at that moment, to indulge it. Sam, in his high chair, was straining to get to the squirrel, and when I asked Luke to get rid of it Sam fell apart. He cried himself out, and then started fussing to nurse— the moment I'd been waiting for.

"Do what you like with our high-strung furry friend there," I said to Luke. "God willing, I'm going to take an afternoon nap with this young man."

To his credit, Luke pulled it together and played with Sam while I got undressed and climbed into bed, then he brought me a cup of tea and tucked us both in. But I could tell he was still worrying about the squirrel, puzzling out what he could have done differently. He took the squirrel outside to bury it in the snow, no doubt with a bloody prayer. I'd gotten Sam down but was still awake when the cabin door burst open again. Luke came into the bedroom and I noticed immediately and with no small degree of irritation that he hadn't taken off his snow-caked boots.

"Sandy," he said, his face alight, "I'm so glad you're still up. You won't believe this."

I was accustomed enough to his enthusiasm to just wait for him to enlighten me, but gestured with my head toward our sleeping child.

"I found tracks," he said, dropping his voice to a whisper. I gave him what could only have been a baffled look before he continued.

"Just down by the lake. I was just going to leave you a note. We'll have to—"

I inhaled sharply as I realized exactly whose tracks he was referring to.

"*Really?*" I said, forgetting to whisper. I climbed out of bed and pulled him out of the room so we wouldn't wake Sam. "Are you *sure?*"

There was surely no mistaking what looked like enormous, bare human footprints, but he had the grace not to point that out.

"By the lake?" I asked. "That's really low elevation, I mean, that's really *close*—"

I so badly wanted to go. I looked at Sam sleeping on the bed, considered calling someone to stay with him. But that would take too much time, and I knew that Luke had already arrived at that conclusion and was just waiting for me to do so.

"I'll call Grandpa," I said. "You go. Just—" and some man-off-to-war archetypal instinct prompted me to lean in and kiss his raspy cheek, and whisper in his ear, "be careful out there, you squirrel-loving madman."

Luke went back into the bedroom and, dangerously, kissed our sleeping baby, then embraced me once more and slipped out the door, pulled it quietly shut behind him. On the spot where he'd been standing, a puddle of snowmelt spread across the floor.

I WOKE, DISORIENTED, TO A fussing baby and snow falling outside. It was dark: the only light was the glow of the wood stove. I slipped away from Sam and lit a lamp, saw that it was just after five. I set about making dinner, figuring Luke should be back soon, one way or the other, and Grandpa had said he'd arrive later tonight. I played with Sam, then got hungry and ate a bowl of the stew, leaving the rest on the stove to keep warm over the pilot light.

A few hours passed, and I put Sam back to bed. I sat on the sofa under a quilt, trying to read, but I kept getting up to check the time, to stir the stew again, to confirm that Luke's flashlight wasn't on the shelf by the door, that he'd taken his pack and all the emergency supplies. I opened the door and stood in the doorway, watching the falling snow caught in the moonlight. A good two inches on the cabin steps that had been clear when I'd fallen asleep. Not a sound in the dark night. My chest tightened, and I felt the first stirrings of real panic.

I called out into the night, listened: nothing. The stew felt leaden in my stomach. I imagined all the things that could go wrong for a man out in the cold, alone and possibly miles from home, and I began to be afraid in a way I'd never experienced. I worried about Sam all the time, but I hadn't even *begun* worrying about Luke; I'd figured I had years, *decades*, before that would become necessary.

The falling snow was hypnotic; together with the moonlight it painted a scene that was deceptively peaceful. I called out again, hearing the strain of desperation in my voice, not caring if I woke Sam. Silence. I shivered in the cold air. I loved Luke too much for anything to happen to him, I *needed* him, his strong gentle presence, his warm and solid and fragile living body. I thought of him wearing Sam in the backpack as he skated across the frozen lake. It had never occurred to me that Luke might be the one to fall.

TWENTY-NINE

A SNOW-LADEN BOUGH HANGS LOW in front of me, blocking my way, and I bash it with my pole. Freed from the weight of snow, the branch lifts high up overhead. I've walked several minutes farther along Charlie's trail before I think to wonder how he got through the obstruction.

I thrust my poles into the snow as I trudge along, using the strength of my arms to aid my progress. The snow keeps falling, and the contours of Charlie's tracks are rapidly losing definition. I try to think of how to use the depth of snow in his tracks to determine whether he's pulling farther away from me as I proceed, or whether I'm slowly gaining on him. I vaguely remember Grandpa elaborating about this very topic, that I would need only a watch, a child's ruler and a scrap of paper for calculations, and I run through possible formulas, sinking gratefully into the distraction for a few moments.

A dark shape on a treetop in the valley below draws my gaze, and I am taken aback to see a golden eagle huddled resolutely on top of a larch. Is it dead, its talons frozen to the bough, or just disinclined to seek shelter? Its feathers are only lightly dusted with snow; surely, if it was cold and dead it would be thoroughly covered, white on white and impossible to see. Or, would it?

I spear my poles into the snow and rifle through my pack for some quick sustenance. My first thermos is empty, and I drink lightly from the second, rationing the sweet but now-lukewarm tea. As though sensing me observing it, the eagle turns its head in my direction. It gazes right through me, unblinking, then lifts off, releasing a shower of snow from the bough. It swoops up through the driving snow, then glides over the valley with more grace than any of us trapped on land could muster.

One spring morning before we had Sam, Luke and I happened upon a display of swallows in a manic swooping dance, weaving close to each other and darting away again in a dense, swirling cloud. I turned to Luke, delighted. He took my hand and solemnly apologized for his shortcomings as an ill-favoured member of the animal kingdom, that he was so woefully unequipped to match or even approach the feat of apparent courtship we had just witnessed. I accepted his apology gravely, but his answering smile had a shadow of regret.

"What great, lumbering beasts we are," he'd said. His eyes were on the swallows; they continued to circle and swoop and dive in their lilting, bat-like manner for the better part of an hour and not one of them ever touched down, and then they seemed to decide as one to leave us, swooping away across the lake.

I squint through the snow, searching, but the dark form of the eagle has faded into the wall of whiteness filling the valley, so I carry on, feeling the distance between myself and everything familiar growing greater with each step.

THIRTY

SAM SQUIRMED IN PROTEST AS I stuffed him into his snowsuit, and my hands trembled as I tried to close the zipper. I managed some soft, reassuring noises despite my panic, and as he began to calm I thought wildly of getting him back to sleep and then leaving him here, alone, cached in the playpen like a fawn under a bush. With unerring juvenile telepathy, he scrunched his face and let out a sustained, piercing wail. I pulled soft boots onto his kicking feet, he took a great gulping breath, and in the moment of quiet I heard Grandpa's truck outside. I peeled Sam out of his snowsuit and tried to soothe him, but, no doubt sensing my agitation, he wouldn't settle. I heard Grandpa banging his boots on the porch and there he was, standing in the doorway of the cabin, his pleased, expectant demeanor at odds with my panic. The snow had stopped, the silence outside seemed to amplify Sam's cries. I told him how long Luke had been gone, and saw the effort he made to temper his reaction.

"I'll go," he said at once, but I shook my head.

"You're a nursing mother, Sandy," he said, tilting his head toward Sam as though that settled it.

And you're, what, seventy-five? I thought, but said, "No. Please. Stay with Sam. I'm ready to go, I—" My voice broke and I stopped, felt that to allow even a hint of grief would be to doom Luke.

He hesitated for a moment, then reached out for Sam.

"The radio phone's working?" he asked, receiving Sam in his arms, then he must have remembered I called him on it this afternoon because he quickly continued, "You go. I'll call someone to stay with Sam and I'll come after you."

I was already pulling my gear out of the baby backpack and stuffing it into the regular one. I pulled on my boots, filled with dread and a desperate impatience. I felt Grandpa's eyes on me, Sam now quiet and watchful in his arms.

"Sandy," Grandpa said, and I glanced at him but then quickly turned back to my bootlaces, unwilling to show how badly I needed the heartening words I was sure would follow. "You'll surely meet up with him on his way back."

On the last words his voice trailed off, so slightly as to be barely discernible, and I felt a sickening lurch in my gut. I tried to conceal my panic for fear he would try again to go in my place and attempted to smile reassuringly, but all I could muster was a weak grimace. I hoisted my pack onto my back, closed the door behind me and rushed down off the porch.

All was silent. If there was any beauty in that night I was blind to it as I ran down the well-worn path to the lake. I called out to Luke, then stopped to listen for a response that did not come. On the edge of the beach I saw Charlie's tracks, and the spot where

Luke's met them. Luke had avoided stepping on them; they were filled with several inches of fresh snow, but unmistakable. I stared at them numbly for just an instant, felt an eerie thrill of fear, then I set off along his trail, running over Luke's boot prints, avoiding Charlie's tracks until the point where Luke had put on snowshoes and started walking over Charlie's trail, and I did the same.

The tracks led away from the lake, up into the old cedars. It was darker under the canopy but the night was bright and I didn't need my flashlight as I moved quickly along the trail. Winding up along the ridge, switching back, weaving along again, the trail keeping a low angle through the trees. Every few minutes I called out, then paused to listen, perfectly still, afraid that the sound of my steps on the snow would drown out a faint cry. I imagined Luke lying injured in the snow as the cold slowly leached his strength, his very life, and I moved faster, sweating under my layers. The trail rose and fell with the lie of the land but never gained the ridge, just traversed northwest, down buried creek beds and back up their other sides, far past the end of our lake. There were still several inches of fresh snow in both sets of tracks, no sign at all that I might be gaining on them. I held on to the fact that Luke had made it this far, maybe he was still going, risking himself to hike through the night, knowing that if the snow kept up the marks of Charlie's passing would be erased by morning.

Breathing hard, I followed the trail as it suddenly climbed steeply up to the ridgetop, then into a small clearing. The tracks swerved around a huge cedar stump and headed steeply downslope. I followed, descending awkwardly, and pushed out from the edge of the forest. The snow had stopped at some point—I hadn't noticed until now. The trail led out onto a low plateau above the frozen marshy area that filled this narrow stretch of valley bottom. A mile off, across the flats, was the back end of our lake.

Numbly, I followed Luke and Charlie's mingled tracks. Out in the open, the wind-affected snow was firm enough, under the thin layer of fresh powder, that I removed my snowshoes; a moment later I reached the spot where Luke had done the same. I felt exposed, and turned on my flashlight. For a few yards of their trail, Charlie's footprint seemed to overlie the marks of Luke's boot but I wasn't sure. I let the beam of my light linger on it a moment, but I couldn't stop. I fought through the tangle of alder and dogwood at the back of the lake and stepped out onto the shore. There was the distant glow of the cabin on the far shore and, at my feet, the tracks led out onto the white expanse of the thickly frozen lake.

It seems to me now that I sensed it before I saw it. As I approached it looked, at first, like a dark thing huddled on the fresh snow. I inhaled sharply and took another few steps, and saw in the beam of my light that the darkness was not a mass, but a gap in the snow. Luke's tracks and Charlie's led straight to it and I followed them, right up to the edge of a large hole, the water black beneath the thin layer of ice that had already formed, sealing it shut.

My mind seemed to stop working as I stared numbly at the hole. I knew that Luke couldn't have just broken through; the jagged chunks of ice frozen in place were far too thick. I scanned desperately for some further sign, but there was nothing. The two sets of tracks, Luke's and Charlie's, led up to the hole, and none led away. I crouched beside the hole and pulled off my glove. The thin sheet of ice covering the hole gave way easily, the water below was dark and frigid. I stood up, ice-cold lake water dripping from my hand.

I did not cry out or throw myself to the ground but closed my eyes. My reeling mind caught and snagged on the idea that if I willed it hard enough I would wake as though from a dream into a summer afternoon in middle childhood. I would be seven years old, looking askance at a skinny boy in cut-off jean shorts. The sun would be warm and the lake calm, the air filled with birdsong. I stood perfectly still while my heart pounded and the cold wind chilled my face, and I don't know how much time passed before I saw the beams of lights on the distant shore and heard Grandpa shouting as he ran toward me across the frozen lake.

PART THREE

THIRTY-ONE

HOW LONG HAVE I BEEN standing here? I look back to see my tracks heavily dusted with fresh snow. I continue, slowly, along Charlie's path through the trees. As always when I think of that night, I can't shake the feeling that I missed some essential clue as I stood on the frozen lake, staring in disbelief at the impossible hole at my feet. Later that night, when Grandpa was questioning me, a thought had flickered past, something Luke said to me after he tracked Charlie alone, while Grandpa was picking me up from the hospital after my appendectomy. *Night was falling, and I knew I should turn back. But the tracks had hold of me, Sandy, in a way I can't explain. If the tracks hadn't stopped, I think I would have followed them forever.* I let the thought slide past, and didn't repeat it to Grandpa, not then or ever.

I step into a clearing. In its centre stands a lone burnt tree, its blackened limbs iced with fluffy snow. Charlie's tracks lead up to and around the tree, then circle back the way they came. As I follow, I have that sense, again, that he's playing games with me, but whether his intent is actually playful or more akin to the time I caught Rachel's cat batting around a vole that hadn't yet realized its impending doom, I have no way of knowing. His trail runs back along the far side of the ridge, parallel to the line of tracks I followed here but just distant enough that they were hidden from my gaze by trees and the slope of the land.

A piercing howl cuts the silence, echoing around me. I stop, heart pounding, and listen. Not quite wolf-ish but deeper, wavering and loon-like. Then, nothing. I think it came from a good distance, but with the way the mountains toss sound around, I couldn't say what direction it originated from. I stand still, waiting for another call that doesn't come. I haven't heard that raw howl in decades and now, even if I get through this unscathed, the only people I could tell are long gone.

THIRTY-TWO

I DUCKED UNDER THE TRAILING cedars and stepped out onto the beach. Six months had passed since Luke disappeared, and the summer sun warmed my exposed arms. The lake was glass; the trees cast effortlessly perfect reflections, and a lone bufflehead drifting near the shore left a visible wake. A good-sized trout jumped not far from where I stood, the spray of droplets briefly illuminated by sunlight. I thought I heard Sam, up at the cabin. His distant cries tugged at me, but I was determined to take a few minutes for myself while Grandpa was visiting. He'd been coming out for weekends once or twice a month, staying in the smaller cabin, and he and Sam were entirely comfortable together.

I stripped off my clothes and reflexively ran my hand over the growing roundness of my midsection. I stepped into the cool water, walked out until the sandy ledge dropped away under my feet and then dove under.

THE FIRST MONTHS AFTER LUKE disappeared had been alternately numb and agonizing, studded with moments of vivid clarity. The whiskey jack would seek me out when I stepped onto the porch each morning. I fed it crumbs from my hand and felt no small measure of relief that some living thing was looking at me the same way as always, as though I were not irreparably damaged. I *felt* irreparably damaged. My only comfort came from escape into books, hot mugs of tea and warm baths; with two of the three at once, I could sometimes manage a moment of peace, but this was rarely possible. There was so much to do just to keep the place going, and Sam always seemed to sleep less than Eva's baby books said he should. Grandpa and Rachel both tried to talk to me about what had happened, about the need to consider making new living arrangements, but I couldn't face it. At that point, to navigate the world without Luke, I needed to avoid looking at his memory and just focus intently on the spaces in between. Like skiing through trees, if I looked at him directly I would come to a crashing, bruising halt.

In the afternoons when Sam napped I would carry him to the beach and stare out at the frozen lake, thinking of great ships taken down by icebergs. I would try to force a smile when Sam woke and turned his face up to mine, his expression solemn and questioning. I was jumpy in the night, flinching at the call of an owl, the snap of a mousetrap. I couldn't get warm; my teeth chattered and my extremities felt numb with cold, no matter how hot I stoked the fire or how many blankets I piled on the bed. I couldn't turn off my racing mind, couldn't sleep under that stack of blankets so heavy they pinned me in place. The most I could do, many nights, was to remain motionless just below the surface of consciousness, not deep enough to dream or even fully sleep, willing myself to sink deeper into darkness and relief but constantly being pulled up to the surface of awareness.

Eventually I would give up, get out of bed and make a cup of tea, stand on the porch and watch the stars or lie on the couch under a heap of quilts, trying to read, aching to feel Luke's solid warmth against me. Some nights Sam would wake, and as I nursed him in the chair by the window, looking out into the empty night, his small warm body felt like the only thing tethering me to the world. I was still in that first ragged aftermath when I became certain that I was pregnant again and I thought, numbly, that now Luke would *have* to turn up, alive and well, because how would I manage without him?

Immediately after Luke disappeared, Grandpa had searched tirelessly along the old tracks for any sign or clue. He found nothing, and when he returned after his last search, when new snow had obscured the old trail completely, he confessed that he believed Luke was in the lake. In late spring, when the ice was finally gone, he called in divers to search its depths. I asked Grandpa what he would do if they found Charlie, but he just shook his head. "None of his kind have ever been found," he said. "I don't know where Charlie is, but I don't believe he's in the lake."

Eva had come from the coast to be there while the divers searched the lake. We both refused to wait up at the cabin while they worked, but I left Sam there, with Rachel and her infant son. Grandpa was out in the boat with the divers, and Eva and I stood together on the beach, wrapped in blankets against the chill like the survivors of a nautical disaster. My sense of anticipation was so acute I could hardly breathe, and I held tightly to Eva's hand. It felt strange to take comfort from her presence, as though I were still a child and not a grown woman who towered over her, but somehow I did. I broke down and wept, and then she did as well, at the horror of it: my love, her son, alone in those cold, dark waters.

What the divers found was worse than finding nothing at all: Luke's backpack, lodged between rocks deep in the lake. Grandpa refused to accept that Luke wasn't there; he paid for a second search the next day, which accomplished nothing. "It doesn't make any sense," he said, exhaustion and strain written onto his face. "Surely, the lake is not so large or so deep that it could conceal the body of a man against such scrutiny."

And so I harboured a kernel of secret, irrational hope, even while Eva and Grandpa accepted that Luke was truly gone. The days lengthened. Sam grew, the baby inside me grew. The sun sparkled on the lake, and I began to swim.

IN OUR NARROW VALLEY THE sun didn't touch the water long enough to really warm it, and it was cool even now, in early August, as I swam out along the northeastern shore. I was far from streamlined but I felt almost as though I'd been briefly, blessedly untethered from gravity. A goldeneye shifted to remain out of my trajectory, its slow, deliberate movement seemingly paced to appear coincidental, as though it wished to avoid me but discreetly, so as not to give offence.

A kingfisher swooped directly overhead to land neatly on a cedar bough, from which vantage she surveyed the water, her fabulous crest giving her an ostentatious air. I sidestroked for a while, watching her. When the kingfisher took off toward the back of the lake, I took a deep breath and dove under again. I couldn't reach or even see the bottom; the lake might as well have been bottomless, a portal into another world I could struggle toward but never reach, and even if I somehow succeeded I could never return. The baby somersaulted inside me and I found myself thinking about in-utero accidents—a cord slipping around a narrow neck, that tangle of vital wires and in the midst of it, the tiny, fragile stowaway.

Grandpa called my constant worrying about the baby "catastrophic thinking" and deemed it a perfectly normal response to sudden tragedy, but I felt it was something more. Luke had worried enough for both of us: I'd always been free to charge full steam ahead. Now, I felt as though I was incrementally absorbing into myself those qualities of his that I couldn't get by without.

I surfaced, felt the sun warm on my face. I followed the shore along to the rockfall, glanced toward our hidden glade and imagined I could detect a whiff of twinflower perfume on the breeze, a faint hint of wild ginger. We'd pulled the canoe over to change Sam's diaper here late last summer, Luke murmuring to the baby, "Son, if these trees could speak, I'd have to cover your sweet little ears."

I left the shoreline and swam farther out into the lake, until I reached the spot where Luke's tracks had stopped at a hole in the ice. My scalp prickled as I thought of Luke reaching up to grab my foot, tug me playfully under as he had when we were children. I braced myself for a moment, treading water.

I dove deep, with a familiar, sickening blend of hope and horror. I imagined my outstretched fingers finding what the divers had missed. I needed proof, to do what I must: gaze dispassionately on my hopeless hopefulness trembling at my feet like something gut-shot, and do it the kindness of smashing its skull. The lake bottom was still far below when my lungs started to fail me and, almost involuntarily, I came gasping to the surface. An osprey called out as it circled nearby, then it tried and splashily failed to make a catch. High above me, I could hear its young calling out hungrily from their perches around the nest, and I turned and swam back across the lake to find my son.

"HOW WAS YOUR SWIM?" GRANDPA asked, handing a blackberry-stained Sam over.

"Good," I said, "warming up. Looks like the baby osprey have their flight feathers."

I helped myself to some of the fat, sticky berries. "Of all our invasive species, the Himalayan blackberry is my hands-down favourite." Even to myself my voice sounded too hearty, false.

"I saw Rachel at the post office," he said. "She said to tell you there are Vaux's swifts nesting in the Anglican church chimney. Says they put on quite a show in the evenings."

"I've noticed. They've been there forever," I said. "And you can tell her I hope she's found someone else to be her new next-door neighbour, because it won't be me. And the two of you can stop conspiring on my behalf, thank you very much."

The life insurance had just come through and I had not a fortune by any definition, but certainly more money than Luke and I had ever had together. I could stay at the cabin, theoretically at least, despite everyone's protests that it was no place for a mother alone with two children. I wanted this baby, but wished that I could have somehow put the pregnancy off for a while, just to catch my breath—perhaps employing the reproductive tactic of delayed embryonic implantation, like so many other mammals around here. I recalled just this sort of muddled thinking from my previous pregnancy, and was reassured that at least that much was the same, because everything else felt different. Different and harder, but to just pack up and leave would have required a deeper acceptance than I could currently muster. I placed my hand protectively over my belly, and addressed Grandpa.

"I'm grateful that you're coming out here so much," I said. "And I know you're probably right, but I can't just leave. I don't know, maybe—"

"Maybe when you have *two* babies out here, all alone?" he asked. "Perhaps *then*, do you suppose? Sandy, if something ever—"

"Something already *did* happen," I said. "And, I know. You're right. Just—" I looked at him, giving up all pretense. "I can't face it, not yet."

"Sandy—" he began, and I picked Sam up and swooped him around, telling him that his flight feathers would soon be in and then I'd have a hard time keeping up with him, wouldn't I? Then there would be blackberry smears all over the ceiling, as well as the floors and walls, wouldn't there? He laughed gaily, and stretched out his arms as I flew him around and around the room.

SEVERAL MONTHS LATER, ON A cold November morning, Sam ran around the cabin, using a chunk of wood from the fireplace as a truck, running it over the walls, the feet of the Charlie statue, the basket containing the birth supplies. I felt vaguely high as I watched him; my head swam and my thoughts were wide-ranging and expansive, as though I'd recently smoked grass—which I most certainly had not. Where was the newborn baby he had been just two years ago? Yes, my son was here with me, but that tiny baby was gone. This busy toddler would disappear, too, and it would be the same with the baby that was due to emerge any day. Each time they changed—from babies to toddlers, to children, teenagers, adults—their previous forms would be lost to me forever, the transformation a kind of disappearance. But, could the reverse also be true? Could disappearance be a kind of transformation?

Sam ran his truck up Charlie's legs and the sculpture's wooden features seemed, for an instant, to waver slightly, but when I looked again they were just the same as always. I felt that peculiar, inner popping sensation I'd experienced only once before and stood up quickly to spare the sofa. I picked my way through the wooden blocks that littered the floor as I walked over to the radio phone, a trail of warm salt water in my wake.

Rachel arrived in just over an hour, and within a few more hours Grandpa had arrived to take care of Sam. I thought, *Everyone is here. Now, surely, Luke will walk through the door.* Then, I was absorbed in the birth and could think of nothing else until she was out, wrapped in flannel and in my arms. I touched her wet, dark hair, looked into her alert blue eyes in exhausted awe. *Lily Eva*, I thought, and searched her face for signs of Luke, of my Grandpa and her namesakes, her two grandmothers. The first snow fell onto the frozen ground, and still Luke didn't return.

THIRTY-THREE

THE TRAIL CONTINUES TO LEAD me back the way I came, neither gaining nor losing much elevation as it traverses the forested hillside. The snow is letting up a bit. The sky is brightening, though in that deceptive, late-afternoon way that will soon give way to the beginnings of dusk. Up ahead on the trail I see what looks like a tuft of fur in one of Charlie's footprints and I rush forward, almost tripping over my snowshoes. My heart pounds at the thought of what this could mean—DNA testing, irrefutable proof and all of the thorny decisions that would go along with that. I am a few yards away when I see that I am mistaken; it's only a windblown scrap of lichen, a dark and hairlike *Bryoria*. When I straighten up, feeling foolish as much as disappointed, my vision darkens momentarily, and I realize how exhausted I am. Out here, tired often means I need to eat; my hunger doesn't seem to kick in during exertion, and I can easily forget to keep refuelling. I dig into my pack for some smoked meat and cheese. As I'm rummaging for the Tupperware, my fingers close on the tiny jam jar of leftover port from Christmas. I swiftly decide not to question what is so clearly the hand of fate, and sip gratefully from the jar. The food and wine clear my mind but weaken my resolve. *This is a fool's errand. What is it that I expect to achieve? Do I suppose that I will come upon Charlie, wrestle him to the ground and force him to tell me his name, to reveal to me the deepest secrets of his nature?* I tip the last sweet drops from the jar. A tree creaks; the sound is uncannily akin to a distant harmonica.

I haul my pack back on, and continue along the path, then stop when I see, up ahead, the place where Charlie's trail turns back on itself, again leading me away from the cabin. He's not walking in circles, exactly, but this roundabout route was clearly not selected for its efficiency at arriving anywhere. I almost feel that I could concede now, just turn back and walk quietly home, if only I could be absolutely certain that Charlie walking through my front yard this morning has nothing to do with Luke. But always, it circles back to Luke, the lost, irretrievable man at the heart of my personal rosary. Luke and Charlie, Charlie and Luke. The cursed, blessed pair of them.

THIRTY-FOUR

EVA, LOOKING PALE AND THIN, came out to meet her new granddaughter a few weeks after Lily was born, and returned for a weekend every month or so, when she could get away from work. She was easy with the baby, but with Sam there was a new unsteadiness. She'd come for a weekend in early March, and while I was putting Lily down for a nap Eva snuggled up on the sofa with Sam and began reading to him from a picture book. When I came back into the room she was weeping silently, an oblivious Sam still chattering to her about the book. I went to her, touched her arm and she looked up, her face stricken.

"I'm sorry, Sandy," she said. "I was starting to think I would be okay, but it's just—" she hesitated, stroked Sam's hair and looked at me, not wanting to explain in front of him. She dug through her purse and handed me a photo, one I'd never seen of Luke as a toddler. Staring at it, I felt, for the first time, a superstitious twinge of fear at the resemblance between father and son.

She seemed uncharacteristically frail as we walked the forest path to the beach—she wanted to spend a moment there before leaving, but when I offered to give her some space alone, she waved a hand and said we should stay. Lily was silent, wide-eyed in my arms. Sam ran along the edge of the lake, throwing chunks of snow out onto the ice. Eva looked out at the lake, her face grimly set, and shook her head. "If only they'd found him," she said. "I can't bear to think of him, still in there." Sam ran to her, and she scooped him up easily, and I told myself that she was still healthy and strong, but the weight she'd lost from her small frame and the bruised-tired look of her eyes worried me.

It was the last time I would really be with her in person. A friend called at the end of March to tell me she'd collapsed and was in the hospital; she'd been diagnosed in the final stage of an aggressive and deadly cancer. I took the train out with the kids to see her, but when we arrived she was heavily sedated and didn't know we were there. Eva didn't revive in the days we spent at the hospital, surrounded by a web of her friends, and I felt defeated, returning home, as though I'd failed her. Grandpa visited shortly after we did, and reported that she was much the same.

She died in April, and Grandpa came down to meet up with us before we travelled to the coast together for the funeral. It seemed to me that he looked older, wearier, though perhaps it was only from the travel. When Lily started fussing in my arms at the burial, I left Sam with Grandpa and walked off with her. I could see the ocean, far off, and the dark blue seemed to me to be the exact shade of Luke's eyes. Eva could have been a second mother to me—that possibility had always hovered in the space between us, but I was too hardened, even as a small child, to allow it. By the time Sam was born and I was really beginning to know her, it was too late. I walked back to the small crowd around the neatly hewn rectangle in the ground, the exposed dirt stark and final.

I would like to say that, in saying goodbye to Eva, I also put to rest any lingering hope that Luke still lived, that I cut loose that spectre and set it adrift over the closely shorn grass, toward the distant, roiling waves, but I did not; I did not even try. Instead I returned to my cabin and carried on as I had, submerged in the work of keeping Sam and Lily fed and clean-ish, stimulated and reasonably safe. I went to town once a week, to shop and do some of the laundry, as handwashing it all was becoming increasingly untenable. We sometimes visited with Rachel and her toddler, Tavi, and Grandpa came down to see us when he could, but it was mostly just me and the kids. Between the lack of adult company and the mundane small adversities of cabin life—keeping the laneway plowed, toilet training with only an outhouse—my thoughts grew circular and self-referential. As I tended my small, determined garden, I had to steel myself to thin the carrots that I couldn't help but think of as babies. The actual babies would catch colds and I'd decide to make elderberry syrup from the tall bushes by the roadside, and the gentle precision of coaxing the berries from their stems was like plucking nipples from the mouths of satiated, sleeping infants. One day as I sat nursing Lily on the front porch, a doe stepped out to the edge of the clearing. She watched me, her gaze alert and steady, and it was a moment before I saw her nervous fawn a few yards behind her, camouflaged in the dappled light. *Aha!* I imagined her thinking, *They* are *mammals!* I began to think that perhaps I should consider moving to town before I lost my mind completely.

LUKE WAS NEVER FOUND. THE spring that Lily was two and Sam was four, the house next door to Rachel's went up for sale again and I surprised myself, as much as anyone, when I decided to move to town. Sam could start school in the fall, and we would still be nearby enough that I could bring the kids out to the cabin on weekends as often as possible. There were stores within walking distance, a school, neighbours. Rachel's son, Tavi, was halfway in age between my two, a perfect intermediary. And as Rachel had pointed out, the church across the street was home to a colony of Vaux's swifts that enlivened our summer evenings with their displays of synchronized aerial acrobatics. Once the kids were down for the night, Rachel and I would sit together out front, chatting and watching the evening's next performance: the emergence of the bats.

At first I couldn't sleep; the streetlights and traffic noise, even in that smallish town, were too much. I put up blackout curtains but then it was too dark, not even moonlight penetrated those heavy drapes. On my third restless night in the new house, I took Sam's slingshot and a cat's eye marble, squinted up at the streetlight that shone directly into my bedroom and shot its bulb out. A dog began to bark in the night. In their own homes but ever-alert for a distant signal, each of the neighbourhood dogs raised its voice and joined in the howl.

Sam was enchanted with the doorbell, the mailbox on the front of the house, and the playground at the school up the street, but fearful and suspicious of the flush toilets, the ringing phone, the incessant humming of the fridge. By daylight, Lily seemed to fear nothing, but she was terrified of the dark and prone to nightmares. I speculated that my terror for Luke, during her earliest embryonic existence, had somehow imprinted her with a fearfulness that her adventurous personality would not countenance and that was allowed to surface only in her dreams, as a nameless horror. Rachel listened indulgently to this theory and posited her own: that the child's overactive imagination was, rather, inherited. Obviously.

We had a soft grassy lawn that sprouted snowdrops and crocuses in early spring, a large maple that shaded the house in summer, and a diverse array of songbirds to watch at the feeder year-round. Skunks prowled the town in evening, to the chagrin of dog owners but not us: Lily said the babies were adorable, tripping over their feet as they determinedly followed their mother like a string of striped furry ducklings, and I didn't disagree. Occasionally around dawn or dusk a few mule deer would wander down into town and graze in the grassy churchyard across the street, until one of the neighbourhood dogs approached and they fled with balletic leaps. In winter we could cross-country ski right there in town, and as they got a little older the kids would ski to school, to the store, to the snow-covered playground with its steep hill for sledding.

The town was at valley bottom; it was not uncommon for fog to completely obscure the mountains and I would find myself staring out the window, vaguely disturbed by their apparent absence. It was as though my house and the surrounding neighbourhood had been plucked up in the night and dropped into another geographic zone entirely. When the mountains finally reappeared they might be drenched in rain, or dusted with snow, and I was reassured to confirm that they hadn't left, only demurely hidden themselves while they changed outfits. Everything was easier in town. I suddenly had time to think, the time I'd been secretly longing for, but I found it oddly unsettling. When Lily began kindergarten, I started taking classes at the college, racing out the door each morning to drive an hour for my first class, then racing home again after. Trading off childcare with Rachel made it possible for both of us to attend school part-time, and while I commiserated with her about being overwhelmed, I often, secretly, welcomed the busyness that kept my still-vivid grief, my more far-ranging thoughts at bay.

One afternoon, when we'd been living in town for a few years, I was walking to the store when the smell of cedar washed over me so intensely that I was momentarily stopped in my tracks. It was as though I'd stepped into a newly built sauna or buried my face in a freshly cut bough and I looked up, dumbfounded, to see a logging truck stopped at the intersection, loaded with fresh logs. I was struck with a diffuse grief, and a sense of being somehow displaced stayed with me all day. That night my dreams were disturbed: Grandpa was telling me to get out of bed, to go make myself useful, and then I was running through a forest with Luke; we were children, we raced each other to some hidden finish line. And then he was gone and I looked around and his tracks were not the shoe prints of a boy but of massive, bare feet—enormous, widely spaced— that led right up to me and suddenly stopped.

THIRTY-FIVE

CHARLIE'S TRACKS LEAD ME OUT into a small clearing with a huge stump that looks familiar. I've been here before, though by a more direct route—the tracks had led me here on that frantic night when I searched for Luke along Charlie's trail. My scalp tingles, and I am suddenly cold. Why has Charlie led me back to this particular place, and where will he lead me next? An image rises, unbidden, of the hole in the thick sheet of ice, the water below dark and glistening, and I push the thought back.

I can see where the line of tracks turns back on itself, just ahead of me, but I walk over every footprint regardless, unwilling to stray, even for a moment, from the trail he has laid out. Just as he did the night Luke disappeared, Charlie has passed by the stump, then turned and headed down the mountain.

Partway down the slope a line of squirrel prints intersects with Charlie's trail at a right angle, and then the squirrel tracks stop. On the other side of Charlie's footprint, a pine marten trail appears along the same trajectory. There is no sign of a scuffle, no sign of any change in Charlie's gait. I crouch to look more closely, but there is nothing more to see, no other explanation for the clear marks. A squirrel ran up to Charlie, and a pine marten ran away. I stare at the tracks, trying to work out the riddle laid out before me. My certainty regarding what is possible, and what is not, pushes back at me, but that certainty is growing weak, worn down by persistent evidence. All I know is that Charlie is somewhere on this trail, and if I stay on his tracks I may find him. I look more closely at them. Perhaps he is not too far ahead: the squirrel and marten tracks are shallow and Charlie's are deep, but in all of them there is only a thin layer of fresh snow.

THIRTY-SIX

I WATCHED RACHEL AND TAVI'S cat, Sugar, through my open kitchen window as I washed the breakfast dishes. The blonde Siamese lurked in stalking position halfway up the grassy bank beside the birdfeeder, her hindquarters twitching as she watched an unwary house finch pecking at fallen grain below the hanging unit. It looked like she might manage to get this one and I barely had time to decide who I was cheering for when Sugar took one swift step forward, her body pressed low, then another. She leapt and pounced, and quickly strode off with the limp bird between her jaws. The survivors lifted off the feeder and fled to the forsythia, chirping loudly in outrage or relief or some complex blend of the two. I dried my hands and phoned Rachel; the sound of her ringing phone drifted through my open window.

"It's me," I said, when she picked up, then lowered my voice so my kids, roughhousing in the living room, wouldn't hear. "Here is your horoscope for the day: You are about to receive a gift. It will appear at your front door, and its appearance will bring great dismay to the young householder."

"Crap," she said. "*Another* one? She's getting another bell and this time I'm going to *staple* it to her. Hey, I was just about to call you. Tavi can't go out to the lake with you today. He woke up with chicken pox."

There was a moment of silence as we both considered that Tavi had been over here all afternoon yesterday, and that even though they were already six and eight, neither of my kids had been through chicken pox yet. Rachel hastened to apologize for unknowingly exposing my kids, and I hastened to tell her that of course it wasn't her fault until we laughed and cursed our luck and got off the phone.

Chicken pox. Well. That wasn't so very terrible, I supposed. Grandpa had told me about the summer when I was three back in Ontario, as described to him by my mother. The little boy next door had been my constant playmate until he was suddenly stricken ill with polio and died, just days after I'd been playing with him in the sandbox. My mother had received the news of the boy's death late at night and she'd stood, terrified, in the doorway of my bedroom, watching me as I slept. Making God only knows what sorts of promises and bargains that I will never be able to discuss with her, now that I could possibly begin to understand.

I finished the dishes and started packing up lunch and snacks for our daytrip out to the lake. We hadn't been there since spending a weekend when Grandpa came out to visit almost a month earlier. I'd been too busy with work: I had recently completed my college program to be a lab technician—Rachel's suggestion, after I insisted I wasn't extroverted or personable enough to join her in the nursing program—and had started working at the hospital. I found the precision of the work satisfying. It was like a recipe whose outcome was not the point; my role was meticulously laid out, a sequence of steps that led to a form of measured success each time, regardless of the result.

"Damn, Spock," Rachel had said affectionately, when I tried to explain this to her. But the contrast of my work with the complexities of parenting was refreshing, and I enjoyed the easy camaraderie with the other staff at the hospital.

It became nearly impossible to find time to get to the lake, and now I felt a sweet anticipation to just be there—to fill my eyes with the green of the cedars, to breathe in the cornucopia of scents in the air. I needed to watch the magic of the place break through to the kids, to feel myself flooded with a sense of peace and, truth be told, a note of prideful affirmation in my parenting, at the inevitable moment when they turned to me, wide-eyed with some discovery, their tongues tripping over explanations ranging from the adorably fanciful to the precociously accurate, their eyes shining with a pure, feral delight.

A ferocious growl from Sam, shortly followed by a gleeful shriek from Lily, drew me back to the present. In the living room, Mowgli the man-cub stalked an alarmingly malevolent Little Orphan Annie, preparing to sink his teeth into her succulent flesh, while she rallied the other orphans to hunt him down and make him their newest pet. I listened to hear which of them would prevail this time.

"Daddy Warbucks can't save you now," Mowgli said menacingly, moving in for the attack. He yelped as the feisty orphan girl tackled him and they both fell to the hardwood floor.

"Now you're mine, man-cub," she countered. "From now on you'll be singing your pretty little songs at the end of my leash!"

I packed the food into my backpack while in the living room, Annie taught a feral, suspicious Mowgli how to eat with a fork and knife.

I knew exactly how the plot would unfold. Mowgli would try to become a Civilized Man. He'd sit at the table, gamely imitating Annie in her demonstration of proper table manners, until he realized that the bear sausages the feisty orphans served him for breakfast were all that remained of his dear friend Baloo. Then he'd throw his head back, howling, and run into the jungle, never again to return to the strange and confusing world of men and orphaned little girls. Silently, I would cheer him on his escape, and wish him well.

IT WAS NORMALLY AN HOUR-LONG drive to the cabin, but the car was struggling more than usual with the sustained elevation gain and it quickly became apparent that it would take even longer.

"When we get there, let's have lunch in the observation tower," Lily said. "And let's call the barred owls, and see if they answer."

"I think that only works in the fall," Sam said. "Right, Mom? In their breeding season?"

I honestly didn't know, but Lily declared that she was going to try anyway, and demonstrated her technique until I told her to stop.

"I'm going to catch a beautiful fish for dinner," she said airily. "A nice, fat rainbow, because I'm a good fisherperson, Grandpa said." I smiled, recalling how she'd asked Grandpa why he always said *men* when what he really meant was *people*, and he apologized for his imprecision and duly changed his language.

Lily kept piping up with her plans for our day, but Sam was quieter. He couldn't possibly remember Luke, not really, but I thought I sensed a strain of melancholy mixed into his excitement about our trips to the lake. I hadn't told the kids Luke was never found, just that he had fallen through the ice and drowned in the lake.

I glanced now at Sam in the rear-view mirror: he was half-smiling as he gazed out the window, perfectly content. I thought wryly that Rachel, who had taken a few psychology classes and was always tossing around her new vocabulary, would say that I was "projecting." I remember my mother talking carefully around the issue of my own father, but I hadn't felt the loss of that man I'd never met until much later, and by then I would just shake the feeling off by telling myself that Grandpa was like a father in every way that mattered. He'd been something of a father to Luke, as well: an oddly incestuous result of our closely shared childhood. I glanced back again at the juvenile humans in my backseat: they were foraging for snacks in the seat-back pockets and diligently dividing up their finds.

I decided to stop at the scrubby riverside meadow that marked the halfway point. I was just pulling over, noting an ominous clunking around the car's rear end, when Lily remembered that she'd forgotten her binoculars on the porch.

"We're not going back," I said.

"I just *really* wish—"

"Lil, don't!" Sam cut her off, urgently.

She gasped. "I didn't finish wishing," she said, chastened. "It doesn't count."

The kids had gotten hold of my old copy of "The Monkey's Paw" last year, and both of them took the story and its blood-spattered moral, "Be careful what you *wish* for," deeply to heart. They swore never to speak the word again. Birthday candles were out of the question. They refused to pull the Christmas turkey's wishbone; I tossed it into the bag of bones I kept for stock, and the next time I made soup they christened it "Wishbone Brew," cautioning each other not to even *think* about anything while eating it. I understood perfectly; since reading the tale as a child I also felt a stirring of foreboding any time I found myself on the verge of wishing for something. Luke had read it too, but he'd felt no such compunction and his openly declared wishes always struck me as foolhardy, though of course I never admitted to such superstition.

There wasn't much use for binoculars today, anyway. The waxwings had come and gone, as had the brief, vibrant week of the mountain bluebirds. Today there were only small, wary flocks of warblers, and a song sparrow that evaded us for several minutes while we scanned the dense leafy tangles of brush for a glimpse of it. A pair of dippers called out gaily to each other as they popped in and out of the clear stream. The clouds were foreboding and the sky was growing ominously dark.

I was impatient to get to the lake, but the kids couldn't simply get into the car; they had to stand at the roadside, thumbs out, so that I could stop and pick them up, asking them where they were headed while they conveyed their surprise and gratitude that I'd bothered to stop for a couple of unknown hitchhikers.

The rain started, a light drizzle, not long before we reached our destination. We pulled off at the unmarked laneway, and I unlocked the gate so we could follow the dirt road to the lake. The narrow laneway felt intimate, welcoming, and I breathed in the scent of skunk cabbage that wafted up from the huge plants lining the creek. Near the end of the laneway, a cloud of swallows swirled past the windshield, and my breath caught. I glanced back and the kids were watching, wide-eyed, as the birds whirled away to safety from the elements.

I parked the car and the kids piled out, grabbed their minnow nets and ran down to the beach ahead of me. I was buoyed by the scent of the cedars and hemlock, the gentle descent along the soft, worn pathway. I felt my steps lighten, my stride lengthen. The kids' voices grew louder as I stepped out onto the beach. Today, in the gentle, persistent rain, the lake seemed empty, quiet. Grandpa and I had decided against any kind of memorial stone for Luke. We had agreed, though without meeting each other's eyes, that the lake itself would serve as the most appropriate marker. I stood at the shore, looking out across the water. Rippling circles from the raindrops blurred into each other on the otherwise calm surface. No ducks, no sign of the eagles or osprey or herons. Just a few indomitable chickadees calling out from the western shore, showcasing their unflappability in the face of any weather condition the latitude and altitude could conspire to conjure up.

The old raft rested against the jumble of deadwood at the mouth of the creek. There were gaps where logs were missing and rusty nails protruded in several spots; the thing invited tetanus, if not drowning. The kids clambered around on it as they searched for minnows, their brightly coloured rain jackets gleaming wetly against the muted tones of the lake and sky. Lily called over that there weren't any minnows, and I suggested that they might still be eggs.

"Then where are the eggs?" she asked, and I conceded that they might not even be eggs yet.

Sam wanted to hike out past the far end of the lake and into the flats, but grizzlies frequented that area at this time of year. I wondered if a grizzly might project its own species' fierce maternal instincts onto other mammalian mothers and give them a wide berth, a sort of interspecies maternal nod, but I simultaneously recognized the lack of logic in my hypothesis. It was spring; the half-starved sows were likely gulping down tender newborn ungulates in full view of the panicking does.

"Mom!" Lily interrupted my thoughts. "Sam says male grizzly bears sometimes eat the cubs. He's lying, right?"

I shot him a glance: *Thanks, Sam!* He continued searching for minnows while I tried to evasively explain away the concept of lactation-suppressed estrus as an incentive for infanticide to my nightmare-prone six-year-old. Really, I shouldn't have bothered; I could easily have denied it and Sam knew better than to press the point. Whether he got that macabre bit of information from Grandpa or from my effusive British babysitter, David Attenborough, I could only guess.

Most likely Grandpa was to blame; we'd agreed to let the children believe, for now, that Charlie existed on these lands only as a wooden sculpture, but we were each periodically guilty of overcompensating for the deception by answering their other queries with a scrupulous, debatably age-inappropriate honesty.

The rain fell harder. After eating our packed lunches up in the covered observation tower, we followed the trail deep into the forest, where it barely penetrated the canopy of old cedars, several of which had fallen across the trail and had to be climbed under or over, depending on their girth and the size of the hiker. Brilliant green moss blanketed granite outcrops; trilliums popped out here and there, and clusters of half-uncoiled ferns. There was a rich, botanical scent of decay in the air, intensified by the rain that dripped through gaps in the trees. The kids ran ahead on an open stretch and Sam called back to me.

"There's something dead," he shouted. My heart seized momentarily and I ran forward. I saw the mid-sized, furry body below the trail before I caught up with them, and stepped down the bank to where they crouched over a lynx. It looked pristine; its blank eyes and absolute stillness contrasting with the living richness of its luscious coat. I touched the long tuft of fur that tipped its ear, couldn't resist stroking it. Its body was stiffened but, as yet, it smelled of nothing but the moss it lay on. I couldn't see a mark on it, but I silently noted the swollen teats.

In all our years living in their prime habitat, seeing their tracks and their scat, this was the first lynx I'd seen, though Luke had once fleetingly glimpsed one. He said it had a ghostliness to it, like the caribou in the dwindling herd just southeast of us: an insular, unearthly quality that makes you wonder whether it is actually a real animal you are seeing. A sudden wave of grief tightened my throat, but when Sam turned from the lynx to look up at me, his serious face and clear blue eyes the image of his father's, I composed myself.

"What happened to it?" Sam asked, looking up at me.

"I don't know," I said. Other than baby birds or small rodents, I'd never come upon something like this, just lying there dead, apparently from natural causes. The forest felt too quiet, and my scalp tingled. If I were a white-tailed doe, this was the moment I would raise the flag of my tail, signal to my young. Then, a soft, distant cry. We all looked at each other, listened. Nothing. Then another mewling cry, not far away. God help me: kittens.

SAM FOUND THE DEN; IT was tucked under the roots of a moss-covered cedar stump. One living kitten—or was it a "cub"?—stared at us, wide-eyed and emaciated. Tiny, it was almost indistinguishable from the offspring of a domestic cat, but the ear tufts and oversized paws gave it away. Its two littermates were very recently dead and had been gnawed on—by their surviving littermate, from the look of the tiny holes. I cautiously extended a hand and the kitten recoiled, then retreated until it backed itself right up against the back of the den. I figured I could brave those little teeth if it resisted, but when I firmly grabbed and lifted it by the scruff it obligingly went limp. The little creature looked alarmingly skinny, and was surely dehydrated as well.

It weighed next to nothing. I slipped my hands around it to hold it more securely, and it didn't fight. Deep blue eyes regarded me calmly, its heart pounded fast against my hands.

"We'll take it with us, and then figure out what to do," I said. Lily was overjoyed, but Sam caught the undertone.

"Mom, we *have* to keep him," he said. "He'll never learn to hunt without his mother to teach him. And look how small he is!"

"We absolutely cannot keep it," I said, in my pleasant-but-firm voice. "But we'll take it with us for now, of course. Let's stop in at the cabin and get some supplies."

I PUSHED OPEN THE CABIN door. The smell of old wood-smoke lingered; everything was just how we'd left it. The counters and table were clear, except for the clean dishes from our last visit, now air-dried, on a kitchen towel. On top of the low shelf, a photo of Luke and myself with an infant Sam sat next to the globe, which rested in the crook of an old white-tail antler that Lily found last spring, on a walk with Grandpa. I handed the cat to Sam while I lit the stove and put a kettle on. The first moments in the cabin, after an absence, always felt a bit strange, my ever-present sense of missing the place spilling over into the experience of arrival.

Lily sat in the doorway, pulling off her hikers. She smiled up at Charlie. "You missed me, didn't you, big fella?" she said softly, and patted his foot. "I *really* missed you. Mama did too, she just doesn't like to say."

Startled, I glanced over sharply, but she was paying no attention to me, just looking affectionately up at Charlie. I filled a bowl with water and tried putting it in front of the little cat, but it shied away, so I settled myself in a chair and dripped water onto its mouth with my finger until it perked up and started licking my fingers with its raspy little tongue. Sam was already rifling through the cedar chest, and brought me a soft wool blanket to wrap the kitten in. I looked through the cupboards in hopes of finding a tin of evaporated milk, but there was only tomato soup and peaches, neither of which seemed remotely appropriate for a not-yet-weaned lynx kitten. Its ribs protruded from its matted fur, and I was suddenly nervous it would die before we could get it to town and feed it.

"Let's get this little one to a vet," I said, and turned off the burner. "I don't think we should wait for Grandpa to drive down, but you can call him and tell him. I'm sure he'll be interested."

I sent the kids on ahead with the kitten, and took a last look at the cabin. "You'll keep an eye on the place, of course?" I said quietly to Charlie. "We'll be back soon." I pulled the door shut, then went around the side of the cabin to shut off the propane, and ran to catch up to my fierce little kittens.

The kids talked over each other the whole way home, trading off "holding the baby" in five-minute intervals. Sam went on about how he'd start hunting snowshoe hare with his slingshot to feed the kitten, and Lily declared that she would make a bed for it, and line it with straw, "just like baby Jesus's manger, where he lays down his sweet head." Her best friend was from a devoutly Catholic family, and she'd been picking up all sorts of things over there.

Then the kids argued over whether the kitten was a boy or a girl, until I told them to stop scrutinizing the poor thing's miniscule genitalia and just keep it warm. It pleased me to think that, whatever happened with the lynx, they would both surely remember this day all their lives. My memories of my own mother made up a slim collection, and I sometimes caught myself trying to stock Sam and Lily up with notable experiences, just in case.

GRANDPA WOULDN'T ARRIVE UNTIL LATE in the evening, so in the meantime we went to see the town vet, who was Rachel's oldest brother and known to us from sharing birthdays and holidays with Rachel and Tavi. Mike, looking unnervingly handsome in his white lab coat, told me cheerfully that the kitten was female and seemed to be in generally good health, though she almost certainly had worms. At this I was distracted for a moment, remembering my mom stopping the car with a gleeful shriek and having me pose with her, grinning, in front of a store's hand-lettered signboard that read, "We Have Worms."

I was smiling—had I ever seen that photo, or just imagined I had?—when Mike looked at me a bit strangely, and I quickly set a more solemn expression so he'd be more likely to think that we would be diligent caregivers for the little scrap. He thought she'd been on her own for no more than a day or two; she'd have died of dehydration quickly without her mother's milk. He dipped a cloth into warmed-up kitten formula, then wiped it against her muzzle. It worked: she licked her face, then took to the rag voraciously.

"I can't say for certain," he said, "but she's probably just over a month old. She should be alright on this formula for now."

It was Sam who broached the question of keeping her; his voice wavered, betraying how deeply he hoped for a positive response.

"I know you would do an outstanding job of taking care of this animal," Mike said, looking at both kids, "but she needs to be raised in a very particular way, so she doesn't get too used to humans. There's a place up north that does that; she'll have to go there. But you two can help make sure she gets her formula until we can transport her."

He looked at me. "Your grandfather's coming, is that right?"

I confirmed that he was, and Mike's nod implied that the arrival of Aidan Fitzpatrick, locally renowned veterinarian, would surely solve not only this predicament but also any others that might arise in the interim.

Relieved of final responsibility, and seeing the kids' reluctant acceptance of his verdict, Mike went on. "I *have* heard of people trying to keep pet lynx," he said. "They seem manageable enough while they're very young, but the next thing you know they're half-grown and the neighbours start losing their chickens and," he glanced toward the waiting room and lowered his voice, "their yappy little dogs." The kids brightened up at the thought of all those toy poodles and chihuahuas disappearing down the gullet of this ravenous little foundling.

Back home, the kids couldn't stop squabbling over whose room the kitten was going to sleep in, so I sent them outside while I made dinner. I put some water on for pasta and then couldn't ignore the poor little beast's plaintive mewling any longer and picked her up. I let her gnaw my fingers and clamber around on me, wondering guiltily if this particular moment was the tilting point when she became habituated to humans and thus doomed, then counter-arguing that there was no point worrying about her distant future if she was to become hypothermic right now. She started sucking on my shirt so I warmed up some more formula, holding her against my chest as I stood at the stove. Her behaviour was really no different than any domestic kitten and I thought, not for the first time, about how everything and everyone starts out completely and unabashedly wild.

I badly wanted to keep this kitten, neighbourhood lapdogs be damned. What was wrong with me? Had I not matured a whit since the age of seven? I thought of that episode of *The Nature of Things* when David Suzuki, politely but disingenuously, asked those Project Nim people what they intended to do once the chimp grew up, and I reluctantly surrendered the kitten to her box. I could not bear even the imagined scorn of David Suzuki.

When I went out to the back porch after dinner, there was the beginning of a glorious sunset over the mountains. The Vaux's swifts were swarming in a tight spiral, preparing to descend en masse into the chimney of the church across the street. All over the neighbourhood, people cracked open cans of beer, flipped sizzling meat on barbecues, called out greetings to each other over their fences. It seemed impossible sometimes, that with all these people within earshot and all the others sauntering around all over the planet, not a single one of them was Luke.

At dusk, Lily came to find me, asking if we were going to watch the bats, and if the kitten could come too. Tiny bright yellow flowers were caught in the dark tangles of her hair—she'd been playing in her "fort," a hollowed-out cave in the sprawling forsythia. I spread out the blanket on the front lawn and Rachel and Tavi came out to join us, the boy, with his red pockmarks, snuggled against Rachel in what we estimated to be a safe distance from my kids, even though we knew they'd already been exposed and it was too late for such precautions.

The kids furiously negotiated possession of the sleeping kitten's box in hushed tones, having been warned of my willingness to put her back inside. The light was growing dimmer, shifting everything from colour into black and white: Dorothy's arrival in Oz, in reverse. The wind was calm, the swifts were done for the night, crows were making their way home. We all watched the patches of clear sky between the maples and oaks, waiting.

"Almost," Sam whispered. A pause. Then I felt as much as saw it, that barely perceptible shift in the light that immediately preceded their emergence.

Lily spotted the first bat. It was small: a little brown or a yuma. It looped quick and swallow-like around the tree, then disappeared into the growing dark. Then another zipped into view to briefly dazzle us with its flying prowess, and another and another, until dozens of bats had emerged from their roosts to zigzag through the evening sky, gleaning insects from leaves, snatching up fluttering moths and eating them on the wing.

Tonight, I would climb into my bed, alone and exhausted as any lone mammalian mother. Tomorrow, or one day very soon, I would awaken to two itchy, irritable children. I tried not to wish things were otherwise. As though reading my mind, Rachel passed me a Mason jar containing a generous splash of Chianti. We toasted. *There may be chicken pox, but there will not be polio.* The lynx would live. She would grow up and, one day, be returned to the lake, to live among the cedars and hemlocks, the snowshoe hares and squirrels, to slink through the snowy forest on massive furry paws, silent as any ghost.

THIRTY-SEVEN

I STEP OUT FROM THE edge of the forest, my knees aching from the long descent. The snow has stopped. An industrious party of pine grosbeaks chatter to each other from a mountain ash. I follow Charlie's tracks out onto the small raised plateau that marks the end of the valley. The hills seem to grow up from this spot in all directions except one; below me I can see the flats stretching out, barren and exposed until, perhaps a mile off, the dense thicket of willow, alder and red-osier dogwood lining the back end of our lake.

I follow Charlie's tracks down along the natural fall line between snow-covered rocks and protruding scrubby trees, and step out into the open expanse of snow over the frozen shallow pond that stretches across this narrow section of the valley bottom. Here in the open the snow is windblown—only an inch of powder remains atop the hard crust. I unstrap my snowshoes and collapse my ski poles, and secure them to the pack. My steps are light and unencumbered and even Charlie's tracks are shallow and suddenly startlingly clear. He leads me on, toward the back of our lake.

I've walked only a few minutes when I come upon a line of tracks that approaches Charlie's trail at a right angle, then runs alongside in the direction I'm heading. I crouch to study the prints more closely and they are distinctly feline. The soft, shallow snow above the wind-crust takes a print beautifully and I can see the marks left by heavy fur on the paws: a lynx, then. The two sets of tracks get progressively closer together, and then the lynx tracks stop. There is only Charlie's trail and, leading away in the other direction, the tracks of a coyote or small wolf. Charlie's tracks continue on toward the lake and out of sight and I accept, finally, that I'll see only what he allows.

I don't realize how long I've been standing there until the cold begins to seep up through the heavy soles of my boots. The numbness in my toes turns to a prickling tingle as I begin to walk.

The bright snow seems to cast its own light. To the west, the mountains and low clouds are tinged pink as the sun descends toward a horizon hidden by endless mountains. It won't be long, now, before this is over.

THIRTY-EIGHT

IN EARLY JUNE OF 1985, the town was scented with lilacs. Even my wild, untended front lawn looked gorgeous, ringed with lupins and wild roses, the overgrown grasses lush and dewy green. I walked up the stone path; a squirrel on the hydro wire above me turned and ran away from the house then back toward it and finally froze, undecided. I stopped on the front step to peer into the robin's nest tucked up high in the forsythia; one of the scraggly nestlings sensed my approach and threw its downy head back. Swiftly, as though not to be outdone, the other three followed suit, their beaks open so wide I could see their pulses throbbing in the tiny purple veins running down the pink lining of their throats. Our calico, Kathmandu, was on her perch on the neighbouring retaining wall, her gaze fixed on the nest, and when I reached the top step she leapt off and ran up the stairs, weaving through my legs as I opened the door.

The front hall was littered with shoes and back-packs, the kids were arguing and the air was sharp with the acrid tang of burnt toast. I'd been enjoying the relative peace and quiet during their last month of school before summer holidays, was just thinking,

Okay, they both made it through another year, and then this morning before work I'd gotten another call from Lily's grade four teacher.

I pushed through the detritus and into the kitchen. The wreckage of their after-school binge covered the table and there was a grilled cheese sandwich burning on the stove. They were arguing over the zip-lock bag we used to store chicken bones in the freezer until we had enough to make stock.

"You can't put those spicy chicken wing bones in there," Sam said as he tried to grab the bag away from Lily. "The flavours are too strong, they'll wreck the broth."

"They're going to boil for hours," she said, glancing at me for agreement as I flipped the burner off. "The spices will be totally worn away."

"Fifty-seventh law of thermodynamics," Sam said, grabbing the bag back. "Flavours cannot be created or destroyed by boiling."

She paused at that, unsure.

"Show-off," she said, and stalked out of the kitchen.

"Keep walking, Lily-liver!" he called out after her, and she gave him the finger as she went out the door. I thought, not for the first time, of how lacking in decorum my home was compared to the rustic but refined world of Grandpa's that I'd grown up in.

I went looking for Lily to ask about her assignment. Her teacher had informed me that her end-of-year project was nowhere near completed; she had started and given up on at least half a dozen ideas, most of them outlandish. I waited for him to tell me something I didn't already know and, perhaps encouraged by my silence, he went on to tell me that her classroom behaviour had been getting worse, she was "no better than the boys." I asked him if he'd called all of their parents, too, all of those boys she was behaving no better than but perhaps no worse than; that query marked the end of any constructive discourse.

Lily was on the front lawn passively harassing the baby robins with her too-close proximity, but she backed off when she saw me.

"They're all still there," she said quickly, and I told her to leave them alone, that from their perspective she was an enormous predator gazing hungrily down on them, deciding which to gobble up first. She looked guilty, and was quite happy to change the subject and tell me about her project, which was now "Can You Change Your Dreams?"

I said it was a fine idea, but asked why she wanted to control her dreams.

"I sometimes have a dream that I can fly," she said. "Not like a bird, but maybe more like being on a trampoline, like the whole ground is a huge trampoline, and so are the rooftops and treetops, and I can push off them and kind of fly, and when I start to come down it's really slow, and I can just bounce off again if I want."

I hadn't had such dreams myself, but agreed that it sounded like a very good time.

"I used to dream about my dad," she said, and when I looked at her, startled, she added, "when I was little."

"Did you?" I asked, keeping my voice light. "You never told me."

She looked at me. "It would have made you sad. That's what he said, anyway."

She watched me, reading my reaction, and gave me an impulsive hug. She cajoled Kathmandu into her backpack and set off on her bike for the library and I watched her, wondering.

THAT NIGHT I WOKE IN the near-darkness to her standing, wraithlike, over my bed.

"Christ, Lily!" I sat up, heart pounding.

She said she'd been trying to catch me in REM sleep, so she could observe me for her project. Apparently, Sam had already kicked her out of his room and pushed the dresser up against his door. I flicked the light on, saw that she was upset.

"Also," she said, "I had a bad dream. A *really* bad one. Can I sleep in here?"

Her lip quivered, and I felt a rush of love for the poor little beast. I pulled back the covers and she climbed in. She fell asleep quickly, her warm little body nestled against me, her loose brown curls spread over my pillow. Even at their age, I still loved my kids the most purely when they were sleeping, perhaps because all my worries about them, for them, faded. She was right here, nothing could happen to her, and Sam was likewise safe behind his barricaded door. I thought about her project—the sweet, naive futility of it. I knew something about wanting to control dreams. I'd tried that just about every night for years, but to no avail. I'd never caught Luke except in fleeting glimpses—he would slip across a forest path, or I'd catch him in my peripheral vision at the roadside as I was driving—other than those rare, impossible to predict but always welcome occasions when I dreamed that we stood silently on that starlit rise of land, the unbroken expanse of snow around us, and he met my gaze but wouldn't explain, wouldn't speak a single word.

It took me a while to fall back asleep after Lily climbed in with me, then a wailing siren woke me an hour before my alarm and again I couldn't get back to sleep. I made myself a coffee and sat exhaustedly on the porch, watching the chickadees and finches on the feeder and admiring the forest garden I'd built in the shade of the retaining wall my first summer here. I'd gathered and dug up various favourites from the forest around the cabin each time we went back there to visit, and transplanted them here in town in an effort to assuage my acute homesickness. There were mossy chunks of decaying wood, delicate maidenhair ferns that had proven surprisingly hardy, and wild ginger that spread a bit each year, slowly filling in the gaps. It was their scent, as much as their appearance, that I found most restorative: I needed only close my eyes and I was back on the land, at least until the next car drove by, or a passing neighbour asked me why I was stretched out on my front lawn with my eyes closed.

Kathmandu was lying in the tiny strip of early sun on the sidewalk and I saw her perk up, her gaze fixed on the long grass across the street. She flattened herself to the ground and began to creep toward it; she'd reached the edge of the pavement when I heard a car. I stood up and frantically called her and, being a cat, she ignored me and continued stalking out onto the road. I ran toward the street but couldn't get there fast enough and then the car was on top of her, over her. It stopped on the road just beyond, the screech of its brakes hanging in the air.

Her eyes were open and full of dust, her skull dented and her intestines coiled wetly on the road beside her torn abdomen. She looked gut-shot and an image instantly came to mind, unbidden, of the snow-shoe hare I'd once inexpertly killed. A middle-aged man I vaguely recognized walked back from where he'd stopped his truck on the street and I reassured him, no of course it's not your fault, thanks for stopping, and he stood guard over her while I went inside for a blanket and scooped her carefully into it. Then I walked slowly toward the house, thinking that the kids were going to wake up any minute and I needed to clean the blood off the road before they saw it, and then I'd have to tell them. I paused on the top step and the mother robin at her nest turned and looked at me, an earthworm dangling from her beak, her open-mouthed babies squawking bloody murder.

THE KIDS DIDN'T PUSH WHEN I told them I wanted to clean her up a bit before they saw her. I cried as I washed her; in death she was so small, so pitifully ruined. I stitched her abdomen closed so she'd be presentable for her wake, and as I pulled the thread through her cold skin I grieved for her bright, focused spark of innocent predatory life, felt guilty that I'd failed to keep her safe even for her relatively short life-span, that I'd gotten her fixed before she could have even a single litter of kittens, that life was too fragile and unpredictable to be borne.

I called Grandpa, to invite him to the funeral. I first asked him how he was doing, a reflexive question. There was a full pause, then he said he was actually rather tired. He'd never said that before and I waited for him to say more and when he didn't, when I finally replied, my voice shook slightly.

"You mean—just normal tired, is that what you mean? Is something wrong?"

"Sandy," he said, "nothing has to be 'wrong.' I am eighty-six years old, my body is staging a dozen tiny rebellions—"

He had clearly intended to go on, but he stopped there.

"What do you mean, rebellions?" I asked, alarmed. "Is there something *wrong*? Should we, I mean, are you supposed to be *doing* something, getting some kind of *medical*—"

He cut me off. "Sandy, please."

I didn't want to hear this. I needed him; the kids needed him. Not to do anything, but just to be himself: alert and energetic, willing and able to discuss any topic—ethical, philosophical, scientific—the three of us could come up with. That he would be healthy and strong at his hundredth birthday was a belief I had held for so long, and with such certainty, that I had long since forgotten it was anything but pre-ordained fact.

"Maybe you should get a young girlfriend, or something," I said.

"Good Lord, Sandy," he said. He *had* dated someone, a colleague, several years back, but it hadn't lasted. He'd told me it had been a nice idea, but he was too old to adjust his habits to those of another person.

I told him about Kathmandu, said he didn't need to come if it was too much trouble. He said of course he'd come, but he couldn't leave until tomorrow afternoon.

I eyed the towel-shrouded bundle uncertainly.

"Okay," I said. "Sure. Tomorrow evening, then."

I opened the freezer and rearranged the bags of frozen vegetables and perogies, the broken popsicle tray and zip-locks full of chicken bones seasoned with spices that might or might not shift the tenor of my next batch of broth. Then, I placed the bundle containing Kathmandu into a plastic grocery bag, and slid her in back.

WE HAD THE WAKE AFTER school on Thursday—neighbourhood children trailing through the front yard where Kathmandu lay on her favourite cushion, her dark fur tipped with frost as she slowly thawed. Rachel and Tavi brought roses from their yard and laid them beside her. Their cat, Sugar, approached Kathmandu, but anyone hoping for a touching display of feline grief was to be disappointed, as she took a cursory sniff and then sauntered off, tail held high.

Grandpa officiated the burial, which was to be a family-only affair, and I reassured myself that he looked the same as always. Lily carried Kathmandu to the backyard and placed her into the hole we'd all taken turns digging, and her effort in keeping composed tore at my heart.

"She was a fine cat, a fine soul," Grandpa said. "May she dream of three-legged squirrels, and birds with broken wings, and the family who loved her so well."

He was so much in his element that I could almost see the priestly robes on him, though of course he'd never worn any, having left the seminary before ordination. I made myself look objectively at my grandfather. He looked tired, and he looked old. I felt a deep, premature grief welling up, and turned away.

IN THE MORNING SAM CLAIMED to be feeling unwell, but he wouldn't meet my eye as he described an unlikely combination of symptoms. My first response was irritation, but I checked it, and decided to call in sick, take him up to the lake for the day. Grandpa had to head home, and Lily was off to school, so it was just the two of us.

Sam was quiet on the drive. As we pulled into the laneway, the sound of the creek and the scent of skunk cabbage wafted into the car. I eased the car around the potholes and stopped at the parking spot. He wordlessly got out of the car, headed for the trail to the lake. I walked up to check on the cabins, sat on the porch for a bit, then followed the worn path to the lake. Sam stood on the beach, looking out at the water. My heart clenched; he looked newly alone, strong and vulnerable at once. I kicked the rocks a bit as I approached, so as not to startle him. I put my hand lightly on his back, and he turned to me, his face crumpling, and collapsed against me, crying. I held him, my first-born, his rapidly changing body both familiar and not. It seemed like only a few years had passed since he ran to me with every small hurt, piled into my arms as though they were his one and true home.

The racking sobs stopped as abruptly as they'd started and he pulled away, roughly wiped his face. After a while he kicked at the pebbles, then skipped a stone, and another. I watched him, his easy athletic grace, and felt a familiar twinge of recognition. But when I tried to imagine Luke—warm and solid and right here beside me, watching our half-grown son—I found that my imagination was not equal to the task. Luke had been so young when I lost him and I no longer felt young; he'd been a new father to a baby and I was halfway through raising two children on my own.

The one thing I still wanted, that I could wrap my worn and tempered hopes around, was something that would at one time have been my darkest fear: to find his sturdy femur, or his beautiful skull with its familiar contours of forehead and temples, the bones finally given up by the lake that had washed them clean. I wanted to stand over an open hole in the ground and lay him down—some part of him, at least—in its depths. To fill in the hole, and then to finally walk away.

Sam threw a flat rock out onto the water; it skipped eight, nine, ten times, the circles spreading across the water and blurring into each other, the rock finally sinking far out in the lake. He turned to me, his face alight, his blue eyes, his curling dark hair, his unguarded smile: Luke's. We drove home to a town scented with lilacs in bloom. Kathmandu lay beneath the ground in the backyard, broken but made beautiful enough, and as I reached the top step I looked into the robin's nest and it was empty, the downy chicks flown off into her dreams.

THIRTY-NINE

IT IS NEARLY DUSK. CHARLIE'S tracks lead me on toward the thicket that separates the flats from the back of our lake. There is another gap in his footprints, this time filled by the small prints of a squirrel, for ten yards, fifteen, twenty. Then, again, Charlie. I keep walking. Farther on, the tracks of a snowshoe hare approach Charlie's, but its tracks stop when they meet up with his. The tracks that emerge on the other side are the neat prints of a deer.

Come and get me, Charlie. Touch me, and decide what marks my next steps will leave on this thin snow. So often, change has come swiftly and with little warning. One moment I was a beloved daughter, an instant later I was an orphan. One morning I woke as a maiden; that very night I fell asleep with my lover. One day I was a wife, and then I was alone with a child, with two children. Each time great change landed swiftly I was so stunned, so foolishly taken aback; as though I was the first to experience such transformation, as though it were not the most natural thing in the world.

FORTY

I HAD NO SENSE OF foreboding, no premonition as I picked up the phone that day in January. It was a Saturday morning and between Sam and Lily's friends and their girlfriends, the phone was in such high demand that I often felt like an unpaid and poorly dressed receptionist for my teenaged children.

"Hello, Sandy Russo?" When I warily agreed that yes, I was she, the woman continued, speaking so quickly I couldn't quite follow. "I'm so sorry," she said, "this is the neighbour." I didn't recognize her voice and tried to think which of my neighbours she was, why she was sorry, but she hurried on.

"I am so sorry," she said again. "I just went over there and I found him, and I knew you were his only family, your number was on the fridge." I gripped the phone, felt suddenly frozen. Not *my* neighbour.

Grief was a distant cloud, darkening the horizon as it swirled closer, and I numbly raced against its advance. I walked to the front of the house, lowered my voice so the kids wouldn't hear me, if they were awake.

"My grandfather," I said.

"Yes," she said. "I'm so sorry. My kids were the ones who noticed something was wrong; it snowed the

night before last and just now they came and told me
there were no boot prints on his walk, and of course
he goes out walking every—" She stopped. I found out
what I needed to, thanked her and got off the phone.

She'd found him in his chair; the lamp was on so it
would have been evening. Slipped away in the night,
while snow fell steadily outside his windows. I sat down
heavily, and lowered my head to the table. *Impossible*,
I thought numbly. *He is supposed to have another eight
years. At least.* My grandfather; their great-grandfather.
Ninety-two years old.

I walked out the front door and stood in the yard
and at the touch of the icy wind my grief was shaken
loose and I wept, the tears warm and then cold on
my face. I tried desperately to soothe myself with
the thought that his death had been kind, arriving
stealthily without the fear or pain it so often accom-
panied. This grief was a child, though, unable to feel
gratitude for how much time I'd had with him, or the
manner of his death, or anything else.

A northern flicker hammered on a hydro pole; a
trio of crows fought over something on the road. The
yard was covered with the tracks of neighbourhood
dogs and cats and the rock doves that hopped around
under the feeder, picking up the fallen seeds. I felt my
shoulders shaking, my teeth chattering. I stomped my
feet to warm up and startled a fox sparrow from the
feeder—it darted back to the safety of the thicket.

A few weeks ago, after Grandpa's last visit, I hugged
him goodbye at the train station, and he spoke the last
words I would ever hear him say. "Take care of our
friend up the mountain," he whispered. He winked at
me, and walked toward the platform.

Sam and Lily were both inside, and they didn't know yet. I weighed out my grief, put most of it aside for later. I walked back into the house, and woke up the kids.

AT THE WAKE, I STARED at his coffin and thought, *It needs a yoke*. If it had a yoke I could lift it up and portage it, just as he taught me. I would bend at the knees and lift it onto my thighs, then swing it up into position above my lowered head. The smooth yoke would settle comfortably onto the back of my neck, I'd brace the gunnels and take one careful, plodding step at a time until I'd gotten him to wherever he needed to go. Someone touched my arm; I didn't look to see who it was. My heart pounded and there was a roaring in my ears, drowning out the keening bagpipes. I straightened up too quickly and in front of my eyes everything was darkness. I groped forward blindly and steadied myself on the table in front of me. An open book came into focus, lines of freshly written names, a pen resting in the crease.

I looked down at the memorial book, lay my hand on the cool, dry paper. I rubbed my thumb over the top of the page as though to erase what was written there. Aidan Joseph Fitzpatrick, 1899–1991.

THERE WOULDN'T BE A BURIAL. He'd been clear, long before his death, that he wanted to be cremated, his ashes scattered across the land. He left a letter for me and the kids with the specifics, but I opened it alone—I wasn't ready to discuss those details with them just yet. *Please just allow me to accompany you as you're out hiking on the land*, he wrote. *And leave a speck of me here and there as you go about your journeys. To have spent my life here is more than I ever deserved, and these wilds are the only heaven I need.*

Whenever Grandpa and I encountered something particularly striking—a distant grizzly family foraging on the flats, a golden eagle soaring over a remote peak—his face took on a rapturous expression, features lit from within as he beheld the fresh wonder. He would turn to me, make sure I was paying attention, and then, after, he would let me try to work out why that particular creature was right here, right now, steering me toward a recognition of the connections between everything.

He dedicated his life to standing sentry on Charlie's territory, but also to ensuring that I could identify as many as possible of the living things that could be found hereabouts—preferably in Latin, with at least a basic understanding of their natural histories and taxonomic classification. I was his classroom, his congregation, and, as children do, I absorbed the subtext more deeply than the lesson ostensibly being presented. Long before I was grown, I accepted as self-evident the importance of knowing whether a particular chickadee chattering from the cedars was a *Poecile atricapillus* or a *Poecile rufescens*, because I had experienced for myself the deep satisfaction in that sudden spark of recognition, that acute and particular pleasure of unexpectedly spotting a familiar and beloved friend in a crowd, and joyfully calling out her name.

A month after Grandpa died, the kids and I drove out to the lake with a portion of his ashes in a tin. It was stormy but the wind whipped most of the snow off the road and Sam was a steady driver, so I fought off the urge to give unnecessary advice. He'd been driving for over a year now, but I still found the rare experience of being a passenger a bit unsettling, and I was relieved when we arrived. We didn't keep the lane plowed, with no one living out there, so we parked at the main road. The swirling wind was cold as we pulled out our gear, sorting out everyone's packs and poles and snowshoes. My exposed face and hands were quickly chilled and I just wanted to get into the trees.

"Alright," I said, and looked at the kids. "Shall we get going?" As I spoke, a rogue wave of grief came from nowhere and swamped me. I tipped my head back, closed my eyes and felt a single hot tear escape onto my cold skin. Lily put her hand against my back.

"I can't believe it, either," she said, looking up at me. "I feel like he should be here with us." Lily hadn't gotten my height—likely wouldn't, now—and her small stature made her look younger than her fifteen years.

"We don't have to go all the way up to the ridge," Sam said quietly, not looking at me. "We could just go right to the cabin, if you want."

"No," I said, wind blowing in my face and making my eyes water even more. "It's a good idea, to get up high. Let's go."

We left the roadside and headed up into the forest, Sam breaking trail and Lily right behind him. The trees provided some shelter from the wind; my exposed skin was cold but I was otherwise warm from exertion as we climbed. It was quiet, most of the forest inhabitants sheltering from the storm. An intrepid squirrel railed noisily at us, then froze on a branch as we approached.

I peered at it more closely. "Look, it's missing a front leg," I said.

"Don't worry, little fella, it'll grow back," Lily called out, and Sam told her this was supposed to be a serious occasion. She said nothing, but a moment later, as Sam passed under a snow-laden bough, she reached up with her pole and lightly tapped it, so the clump of snow fell right onto him. He dug the snow out from the neck of his jacket and threw it at her, and she squealed and ducked. When she looked back, I smiled and shook my head with that gesture of affectionate faux-exasperation particular to mothers, to let her know all was well. We'd already talked about this, in the car—that Grandpa wouldn't want or expect too much solemnity on this occasion. "Hey, let me break trail for a while," she said, and Sam let her pass. The wind was strong, and the trees creaked and shed clumps of snow as we continued up. We'd planned to keep most of his ashes for hiking season so we could access all his favourite spots, but none of us wanted to wait for spring for the small ceremony of his "first scattering." We'd discussed a few options, then Lily suggested we climb high above the lake and cabins, so that the snowmelt would carry the ashes down across the land before it reached the lake, which led to the creek, which eventually continued downstream to join the river—and eventually, we could only assume, the ocean.

We gained the ridge, then followed it until we came to the small clearing between closely spaced trees where we'd once sheltered with Grandpa during a sudden rain shower. I dug the tin out of my pack and Sam reached for it but then stopped, looked at me uncertainly.

"Why don't we each pour out a bit," I said, and we crouched in a tight circle to block the wind. I dug out a small hole in the snow with my gloved hand, and tipped a bit of the ashes into it, then passed the jar to Sam, who followed suit. Lily tipped out the final bit, and the wind took the last fine dust from the tin. We stood, and I pulled a folded piece of paper from my pocket. The wind tugged at the sheet, and I tried to keep my hands and voice steady as I read the Emerson quote that Grandpa selected for the occasion.

I sprinkled a bit of fresh snow over the pile of ashes, and the kids did the same until there was a small heap of snow marking their great-grandfather's, my grandfather's, long life. It was too cold to linger and I told the kids to start heading back. I held back a moment, watched the relentless wind tear at the fragile cairn. Then I packed away the tin and followed my children down the mountain, the quote I'd just read playing over in my mind: *It is the secret of the world that all things subsist and do not die, but only retire a little from sight and afterwards return again... Nothing is dead: men feign themselves dead and endure mock funerals and mournful obituaries, and there they stand looking out of the window, sound and well, in some strange new disguise.*

WITH MY GRANDFATHER'S DEATH, I lost not only the man who had raised me but also, somehow, Charlie. I had no one to collude with, no one to confirm that Charlie had been here. I considered telling the kids, but as years passed with no sign of the creatures and credible reports of sightings in the area dwindled to nothing, I waffled, told myself that the question of disclosure had likely become moot. I left them a sealed note in my will, just in case, and kept waiting for the right time. Sam graduated high school, then Lily, and I moved back to the cabin, commuting to the hospital and back every weekday. I stay in town occasionally, to see a show or just visit with Rachel, but my heart still lifts each time I leave the main road and turn onto our lane.

Almost a decade has passed since I moved back here. The kids visit, when Lily has a break from wildlife research, when Sam isn't treeplanting or ski guiding, but when I am not at the lab I am usually home, usually alone. I dated occasionally, while living in town, but I stopped entirely when I moved back. It wasn't about Luke, though I know that's what Rachel and the kids think. There just isn't anyone I want to be here with, and I need to be here more than I need to be with anyone. I'm not lonely, though I've given up trying to explain that to anyone.

I've been here through the long, warm days of summer, with enough light for berry picking and fishing after work, and I've hauled firewood through the cooling, shortening days of autumn, while mushrooms seem to spring up beneath my feet in the damp forest. I've weathered the winters, when everything that walks leaves its tracks clearly on the land and the lake, and each year welcomed the melting into spring, when the lake slowly thaws from the outside in, the Douglas firs gaily paint their nails pink and migrating mountain bluebirds perch on treetops, the males dazzling in their brilliant plumage.

I've settled into the comforting rhythm of the seasons, accepting gratefully those occasional gifts that come to anyone who lives in a place like this. My first summer back, a goshawk allowed me just the briefest glimpse of its muscular profile as it swooped through the forest. During my second or third winter, I caught a breathtaking glimpse of a lynx as it crossed the trail far ahead of me, so ghostlike that I would have thought myself dreaming if its passage wasn't confirmed by the tracks in the snow. Five years ago, I was drinking my morning tea down at the lake when I spotted a flash of bright yellow, bumping up against the driftwood that clogged the mouth of the creek. I waded in and pulled out a child's plastic shovel, a long-lost relic of my grown children's childhood. It reassured me that even a small lake, like mine, has secrets that it will capriciously guard or reveal according to no schedule but its own.

The year before last, a lone heron stayed behind late into fall, then early winter, as the lake began to freeze. It stared at me listlessly as I approached, and it didn't fly off even as I watched it at length. I looked for it each day—checking my impulse to capture it, bring it indoors and nurse it through its dotage on pet-store guppies—until one morning I found a long, frost-tipped feather lying on the ice, and no sign of the bird itself. And one crisp morning just a few weeks ago, I was tidying up the cabin when I was sure I heard the door creak open. I looked over sharply, and the door was open just a crack. I walked over, heart pounding. I peered out but there was nobody there, not a mark upon the fresh snow.

All those years and no sign of Luke, not a scrap of fabric, not a single bone washed up on shore. No sign, either, of Charlie, nothing to suggest that any of his kind might still walk the mountains surrounding the cabin. Finally, this morning, I stepped out of my cabin to see Charlie's clear tracks in the snow. I crouched down to examine them and a whiskey jack watched me, intently. As though I might unearth something that would be of interest to us both.

FORTY-ONE

NOW, IT IS DUSK, AND stars I can't name appear in the darkening sky. Three pale, drowned fir loom overhead, ghostlike in the low light. I begin to push through the dense, tangled thicket, snagged and whipped by branches. Perhaps Charlie waits for me on the other side. Or, only an endless line of tracks that I could follow forever and never catch up to him, never look in his eyes as Grandpa had, in 1920. As Luke surely must have, in the end. I have always imagined that Luke was stolen from me, *taken*, either literally or through some intangible, impossible process. Perhaps I've been wrong, all along. Perhaps, in the end, it was Luke who reached out his hand.

I push through the last of the tangled brush and step out onto the back end of the frozen lake. The ice is intact, but Charlie's tracks lead toward the place where, once, a large jagged hole had been. I walk slowly alongside as his tracks stop and those of a hare fill the gap before Charlie's begin again. After a few yards, they are briefly replaced by those of a lynx. Farther along, the lynx tracks stop and a caribou seems to have appeared from thin air, walked for several yards along Charlie's trajectory, and then vanished before Charlie's large feet again left their marks in the snow.

At the very place where the hole had been, there is a set of footprints side by side: impossibly huge, but more or less the shape my own tracks would be, if I'd foolishly wandered out in bare feet. Beyond those, nothing. It is as though Charlie stood briefly at attention, then lifted off. Inside the prints, the faint dusting of snow is soft and undisturbed, except for a dark smudge inside the imprint of his left foot.

A Steller's jay flies over me, dark against the sky. It calls out in its rough voice and disappears into the trees. From the western shore a raven calls out, an odd gurgling croak, and is answered by another across the lake. A flock of pine siskins passes overhead; their chirping increases in volume, then fades off as they disappear over the ridge. There is a flash of movement at the forest edge and I turn to see a whiskey jack as it settles on a cedar bough, releasing a tiny shower of snow under its meagre weight. I pull off my gloves, then crouch before Charlie's left footprint and reach for the dark smudge inside it. My fingers close around a small, grey feather. I stand, cup it in my hands. It is soft against my skin and seems, for just a moment, to carry a warmth that swiftly dissipates in the cold air. I look to where the bird was perched but it has flown deeper into the trees, into the great wild heavens.

ACKNOWLEDGEMENTS

MANY HEARTFELT THANKS TO EVERYONE at Douglas & McIntyre; I couldn't have asked for a more skilled and supportive team. I'd like to particularly thank Anna Comfort O'Keeffe for her keen vision, insight and sense of humour. Special thanks also to editor Pam Robertson, who whipped the manuscript into shape with cheerful precision and deep understanding, and copy editor Emma Skagen who similarly worked her magic graciously and efficiently.

I want to thank the various members of the Nelson B&I writing group during the lengthy stretch of time that I worked on this novel: Vangie Bergum, Jane Byers, Jennifer Craig, Anne DeGrace, Rita Moir, Kristene Perron and Verna Relkoff. The early drafts of this novel would have languished indefinitely without your generous encouragement and practical assistance.

Room Magazine, when they were still *Room of One's Own*, published my first short story back when I was a camp cook in northern Ontario. That story was, in some ways, the seed for this one, and a few fragments found their way into this book.

Rayya Liebich and Melissa Owen provided valuable and enthusiastic feedback on an early draft and were unfailingly supportive throughout this process. Andy Butler, Steph Butler, Dan Butler and Peggy Collins very kindly fielded my inquiries into their various areas of expertise, and Marg and Pete Butler advised on matters ranging from gardening to grammar. Thanks to Judith Robertson for allowing me and my son the use of her cabin for some weekend excursions that provided a glimpse into the realities of off-grid living. And many thanks to Thomas Hill for generously sharing his extensive knowledge of local ecology, and for letting me attempt to be helpful on wildlife research missions across the region. This would have been a different and lesser book without each of you.

I also want to thank my son, K, for inspiring me with his imagination and his wholehearted appreciation of the gorgeous region we are so lucky to live in. And finally, my endless gratitude to troubadour plumber Brendan Geraghty, for always tracking me down and bringing me back to earth.